A PROOF OF TRUTH

— ANNAPURNA SARIPALLI —

Leadstart
INKSTATE

ISBN 978-93-90463-23-7

First published in India 2021 by Inkstate Books
An imprint of Leadstart Publishing Pvt Ltd

Sales Office:
Unit No.25/26, Building No.A/1,
Near Wadala RTO,
Wadala (East), Mumbai – 400037 India
Phone: +91 969933000
Email: info@leadstartcorp.com
www.leadstartcorp.com

Editor: Ateendriya Das Gupta
Cover: Ami Parekh
Layouts: Kshitij Dhawale

*To my wonderful children and all those who have inspired me
to be more*

ABOUT THE AUTHOR

A techie once upon a time, who later studied to become a management professional, Annapurna has forever been in search of her true north. Books are her most treasured friends, and they transport her to far-off lands, away from the perils of fussy clients, grumpy bosses, cranky kids, and absconding family members.

Annapurna likes well-made TV shows and movies and is also a music aficionado with eclectic tastes—from South Indian classical music to progressive trance. One sees a reflection of her music choices in her writing. Do plug in your headphones while reading her books and listen to the songs to actually live the character.

A Proof of Truth is Annapurna's first book, which she wrote during her career break, as she reflected upon the various aspects of human life—judgement, relationships, human conscience, familial bonds, spirituality, and most importantly, the indefatigable desire to win at everything.

CONTENTS

⇢— ACKNOWLEDGEMENTS —⇠

Dear Readers

Thank you, thank you, and thank you—for spending your precious time and money on this book. I hope it was worth every second and every penny. And I hope it made you think, muse, imagine, laugh. Most importantly, though, I hope it made you happy.

This book was born out of conversations with my husband, where he always takes the opposing view and a counter-perspective. So, I would like to first thank him for encouraging me to give words to my thoughts. I would also like to thank my two wonderful children, who are adorably loveable and can put a smile on my face even when they are cranky, overtired, mischievous, and petulant. I also thank my father for showing me the meaning of unconditional love and good parenting.

There are a whole lot of other people, including my dear family and friends, who have stood by me during this long and memorable journey. I am truly blessed to have them in my life.

There are few people I want to especially thank, although I am not sure if they would ever read this book, much less be aware of its existence.

The first is Sadhguru Jaggi Vasudev. I have never found anyone as intellectually stimulating or articulate as he is, and I have liberally borrowed from his teachings and good words to use in my book. I hope his wisdom continues to light my world and give my future the direction it needs.

I would also like to thank the celebrated writer George R.R. Martin. His narration style is what inspired me to write this book in dual PoV.

I hope to write more books in the future, and your readership will inspire me to continue this journey.

Until next time.

CHAPTER 1

Ajay

I thrum my fingers on the steering wheel of my Audi A3 in time to the progressive trance playing on the stereo. It's a rainy day in Singapore as I make my way back to my office at Lawson Partners in Panorama City. I steer my car into the parking lot in the basement. It's all dark and silent around me—a stark contrast to my buoyant mood, thanks to today's victory in a longstanding litigation with TechCorp on data theft.

My career as a partner specializing in cybercrime and money-laundering is at its peak, and I couldn't be happier. Our firm is one of the most reputed and sought-after firms in East Asia, and we are planning to expand our offices to Tokyo soon. I am looking forward to this expansion and the interesting opportunities it will bring. As I make my way into my office, Christine greets me with a smile.

"Hello, Mr. Bhargav."

"Hey, Christine. What's up? Any messages for me?"

"Your mother called, Mr. Bhargav. She sounded worried."

Mother had tried calling me, but I was busy with back-to-back meetings. I check my phone and see two missed calls and a message from my wife: "Please call your mum when you find time. Don't worry, nothing serious."

Christine has a steaming cup of my evening caffeine fix ready on my table. I send her away, pick my coffee, and move to the tall windows behind my desk to call my mother. She answers after two rings.

"Ajay!"

The sweet lilt in her voice soothes the adrenaline rush I have been feeling the whole day. I close my eyes, cherishing it. Her voice stirs a longing in my heart that only she can sate.

"Mom, is everything okay?"

She sighs. "Your father's COPD has worsened. We met Doctor Shukla today. He has advised a lot of bed rest and has started some new medication. I am exhausted and worried and can't deal with this alone. We need you."

I want to help her so badly. But my father and I—we have issues.

"Mom, I am the last person who can help. You know this."

"No, son. Your father misses you. He is just not good at showing it."

"Mom, I was there three months ago. I don't think I was missed one bit."

"Ajay, please think about it. Not for your father. For my sake. That's all I am asking."

"Okay, let me talk to Tavishi. But Mom, please, don't stress yourself."

"Thank you, son. Will wait for your call."

I hang up and tell Christine I am done for the day. On the way back home, my mind wanders to my past and my times with my father.

❖ ❖ ❖

I had always been a disappointment to him. He despised my carefree attitude. Control was his middle name, and he ruled over my mother and me with an iron fist. Initially, when I was a child, I tried to conform. But as I grew older, I started to give up. We didn't see eye-to-eye on most things. I loved music, but to him that was a waste of time and he made me discontinue my classes. I loved football, but the sport had no future in our country, and he wanted me to play cricket instead. My grades were good, and I knew I was smart, but I was never top of the class like he expected me to be. I put up with him until graduation and then moved to London to pursue my masters. When I came back, he insisted that I work at his law firm. I relented, hoping to mend our relationship and learn the profession from the best. But I could not tolerate his overbearing ways at work and things slowly got worse. We would frequently bring our arguments home, which upset my mother.

And that's how I was living my life—smothered and train wrecked—until the day I met my wife. The memory of that day still brings a smile on my face. I was down with food poisoning and wanted to take a quick pill before I rushed to the court. I pleaded with the receptionist at the local hospital to give me a slot with any physician, but she would not budge. I was clutching my stomach to push back the pain when I heard a pleasant voice.

"Come with me."

I looked up to see a young woman with thick black hair and a quaint smile. She was beautiful, with clear features and beguiling eyes.

I groaned in agony even as I followed her.

"Shhh … it's going to be okay. Wait here. I will get you some pills. But they will take some time to act, and you will need to rest."

"I need to rush to the court. I have a session in an hour."

"Sorry, but that's the best we have. If you have a driver, you could rest on the drive to the court."

"Okay. Let me try."

I called our driver to meet me at the hospital, while my saviour went to get me my magic medication. She showed up a few minutes later and handed me some pills and water. I gulped them down.

"Thank you, Ms …?"

"Doctor. Doctor Tavishi."

"Hi, Tavishi. I am Ajay."

That was the beginning of our beautiful relationship. In a few weeks, we were madly in love. But I was in for a rude shock when one day, out of the blue, my father announced my impending engagement to the daughter of his business partner. I blatantly refused and put my foot down. He reluctantly acquiesced but showed his disappointment and displeasure at every opportunity he could find. Tavishi's father was a junior employee in the electricity department. For my father, this was a blow to his status. His attitude towards Tavishi was barely civil. When my in-laws visited us a few months after our marriage, unbeknownst to me, my father insulted my father-in-law. He passed a sly remark about Tavishi's family's grand fortune to have got me as a son-in-law, insinuating that they were gold diggers. Tavishi never told me what happened. She swallowed the hurt and insult for my sake. I came to know about the incident from my brother-in-law, who was only watching out for his dear sister. By this time, things had escalated to a point where I could no longer stand to even look at my father. Tavishi and I decided it was best to move out. And that brought us to Singapore.

❖ ❖ ❖

We have been living here for nearly eight years and have built the perfect life. A beautiful home, complete with the flower garden that my nearly four-year-old daughter, Aria, loves. Easy access to a stadium, where my seven-year-old son, Arka, learns football. Fulfilling careers. And a small group of close friends who we consider family.

We have continued the practice of visiting our families in India. But over the years, my father has shown no signs of warming up to us, or even our children. While my mother spends all her time with them when we visit, my father just about tolerates their presence.

⁌ ⁌ ⁌

I think of my conversation with my mother, and I know I have to broach this contentious subject with my wife today. She always wanted to be close to her family, but I had my career so we never really managed to make a decision. Now I am well-settled, but she has just started a new clinic here. I know it will be difficult for her to shift. I know she is going to ask for more time, and I hope I can use that as an excuse for postponing my return to India. In the meanwhile, I decide to visit alone and check on my father.

When I reach home and open the door, I am immediately greeted by a happy squeal. "Daddy!"

I put my lips on my daughter's soft hair and all my worries disappear. I inhale her soothing scent of apples and vanilla—my precious baby girl!

"Hello, sweetheart! How is my princess today?"

"Today, I got new colours at school. Mommy and I are colouring a cat."

"Wow! What colour is the cat?"

"Yellow! Can cats be yellow?"

"Of course!"

"Come on, Arya. Let Daddy freshen up. We will finish the colouring until then." Tavishi walks up to me and plants a soft kiss on my cheek. "How was your day? What happened at the court?"

"All clear. We won the litigation." I hesitate to broach the subject that I must. "Listen, Tavi … there is something … I need to discuss with you. Can we sit after dinner for a while?" I spit out the words haltingly.

Tavishi smiles at me. "It's about your father, right?"

She already knows. I look at her curiously.

"Your mum called," Tavishi says by way of an explanation. "Anyway, dinner is on the table. Arya and I had ours. Arka is now done with his homework, so you boys can finish up quickly." There is a strange excitement in her voice – I can only imagine why. She kisses me softly again before taking Arya away.

These days, there are only two kinds of diet we follow. What my son likes and what my daughter likes. So I am pleasantly surprised when I find a cup of my favourite semolina pudding on the table. But when I take a small scoop, I feel like a sacrificial lamb because everything happening now is deceptively appealing. I brush my thoughts aside and finish my food, almost in a rush.

I put the kids to bed and head to our bedroom. My wife is in the balcony, looking poignantly at our garden. When I approach, she turns, hugging me close and resting her head on my chest.

"I want to go home."

"What?"

"I want to go back to India, Ajay."

I lift her chin and look into her eyes. Have I been missing something?

"Tavi, what about your clinic here? And … my father?"

"The clinic is up and running. Chen and the team can manage it. Strictly speaking, they don't need me. And as for your father … it's in the past. What's the point of holding on to it?"

"Tavi, I'm not sure. This is all very sudden."

We move to the lounge chairs, and Tavi nimbly settles down on my lap.

"Ajay, listen to me. We don't belong here at all. What do we have here? Only some friends we call family. But our real family is there. We need them. They need us. All along, I have missed them, but I have been ignoring my feelings. When I spoke to your mum today and heard the longing in her voice, I knew we must take stock. It's the right time for the kids, too. They have just started the new academic year, and it won't be difficult to adjust to the syllabus in India if we move now. I am sure they will love to be in their country. We don't have any excuses now. Let's just go home."

"All right, but let's give it some time, Tavi. Let's sit on it for a while and then decide. Come on, let's go to bed."

❖ ❖ ❖

It's been three weeks since my talk with Tavishi. I am now on my way to India.

When we proposed our plan to the kids, they were pretty excited, so it became an easy decision to make. I transferred my pending cases to my firm and was glad they could relieve me so quickly. I still have some stuff to close, so I've promised to come back and deal with them as soon as I can. Tavishi will join me in India a week later, after shifting our furniture and taking care of some pending stuff. We are going to move to our flat in Mumbai, closer to my parent's home.

As the flight attendant announces our landing in Mumbai, I make a wish with all my heart: *This time, maybe I will finally find peace at home.*

CHAPTER 2

Ajay

As I step out of the airport, the familiar scent of Mumbai air hits me strongly. I look at the line of chauffeurs and spot my family driver, Singha. He takes my luggage and guides me to the car that will take us home to Andheri.

Having settled in, I ask, "How are you, Singha?"

"Great, Beta. especially now that you are here. When Madam told me that you were coming back, I was so excited!"

"How is Mom? And Father?"

Singha looks at me in the rear-view mirror with a smile splayed across his face. He has been with us since I was a boy and knows our family well. Perhaps more than I do. Back in the day, when my father would lash out at me for something I did, I would sit quietly in the car and cry. Singha would do his best to cheer me up. His wife, Ganga, is our housekeeper and a companion of sorts to my mother.

"Your father has softened up, Beta. After the last time you left, your mother came down with the flu, and he was lost and helpless. Ganga was away helping our daughter with her newborn son. So your parents were all by themselves. Your mother needed to be cared for, and he did not know how. It feels bad to see how the lion of a man has become a cat."

I understand what he is trying to tell me. I wanted to come and take care of my mother, but Tavi fell ill and I could not travel. Maybe the flu was a blessing. It finally seems to have opened my father's eyes and made my mother more assertive.

I think about my conversation with my co-passenger on the flight here, who chewed my ear off with his stories about his time serving the defence organization in the country. He is retired now, and both his kids are living abroad pursuing their respective careers, with no plans of returning to this country. So when I told him I was coming back to India to take care of my parents, he could not hide his surprise and admiration.

Maybe coming here will not be a bad decision after all. As I think about my parents, I slowly drift off into a deep slumber.

I am jolted awake by the voice on the radio. It sounds urgent. *The case against Kishore Mehta's son put on the fast-track list following a protest by the Nari Shakti group…* The name rings a bell, but before I can ask, Singha announces our arrival.

At the door, my mother greets me with a jubilant smile and engulfs me in a warm hug. She takes me in to pamper me with a rich feast. We discuss our plans for the future, and she is not very happy about my plan to live in a separate house. But she doesn't push it. I know I have to check on my father in some time, but right now, I let her indulge me with her excitement over spending time with her grandchildren without the pressure of a ticking clock. When we're done, I head to my room to catch some much-needed sleep.

Well-rested, I prepare myself to see my father. I head over to his study and gently open the door. He is sleeping peacefully in his reclining chair, his elbows perched on the armrests and palms glued at the fingertips. I gaze at his form. The man radiates power even in his sleep.

Trivikram Bhargav is a force to reckon with. Orphaned at a young age, he was adopted by a childless couple. But he refused their charity. Instead, he took up petty jobs to pay for food and stay, promising to repay the education expenses as soon as he found employment. Brutally hardworking and ruthlessly smart, he aced his studies and rose to the position of Advocate General of the state in no time. But before long, he left his thriving career with the government and started his own law firm, TS Partners, with his college friend Sarvesh. Though not as successful and powerful as my father, Sarvesh was a smart and nice person. I worked with him during my early days at TS on a couple of criminal cases. He mentored me well, and there were no hard feelings when I told him I could not marry his daughter. Recently, he moved to the US for the treatment of his wife, which left TS with no leadership. Everyone hoped I would step in and take my father's place one day.

I take a few steps into the room, closer to his reclining chair, and softly call him.

"Father!"

He immediately sits upright in the chair and looks up at me. "Ajay! You're here! How are you doing? How is everyone else?" I am easily half a foot taller than he is, at six feet three inches, and am literally towering over him. But he is the one who has power over me—even now.

"Tavishi, Arka and Arya are doing well. They will join me shortly. How is your health?"

"Oh, the usual. But doctors are doing their best. Let's hope these new medicines are effective. Your mother is really excited about your return. She has so many ideas for the kids. She even got a small play area installed in our front yard."

He doesn't know yet that we plan to live at a different house. Not knowing how to bring it up, I change the topic. "How is the firm? Is everyone managing fine?"

"They are doing fine. I have offloaded some of my responsibilities to the other senior partners. We will decide on the course of action in the next quarter's board meeting. But there is something I need from you." There is a slight hesitation in his voice as he gets up from his chair and walks to the desk.

"What is it?"

"There is a case that I need you to take up. It's for my friend, Kishore Mehta. It's a sexual assault and murder case, and the accused is his son, Vishal. I would have taken it up myself, if not for my health."

I blink, momentarily shocked by his words. My father has never asked me for help until this moment. The fuzzy voice over the radio about some fast-track list comes to my mind. Kishore Mehta is the biological son of my father's foster parents. After taking my father in, they went on to have a child of their own—very late in their lives. My father was in high school when the child was born. The child grew up to become a successful movie star. I don't remember ever meeting any of them, except when Kishore Mehta attended my wedding.

But ... a sexual assault and murder case involving a movie star's son? Father must surely be joking! I came to India hoping to stay for good, but in this moment, I want to leave this place running. I cannot take this case, so I try to reason with him. "Father, I *just* came here. I need to get my bearings together. I don't know the first thing about the case, and I heard it is on some fast-track list. Besides, the last time I ever worked on a criminal case was with Sarvesh nearly a decade ago.

The client is obviously important to you, and this case needs someone more experienced. I am not sure I can handle it. Maybe you should ask Sarvesh."

"I owe the Mehtas. I owe them everything. My entire life and your life too, by extension. Besides, Sarvesh is taking care of his ill wife. I cannot burden him with this. You will have to take this case. And you are *not* going to fail."

I want to truly believe that *he* believes that. But he is only saying these things to make me agree. Before I can protest, he quickly adds, "Ajay, please. Do this for me. I promise I won't interfere. The case is completely yours. No matter what happens, I won't blame you. This one is on me. I told Kishore the same thing and he agreed."

I am helpless and have no choice—because I can sense the desperation in his voice and because I can never back away from a challenge. I think my father knows it too, which is why he thought of me in the first place.

"Sanjay, from our criminal law department, is already on it. He is a very sharp lad. He knows all the facts. You should meet him to get started. And Roopa will assist you too."

I close my eyes and take a deep breath. The familiar feeling of suffocation subdues me, and I feel a headache looming.

Suddenly, I hear my father's soft voice, "Thank you."

In all my thirty-six years of life, I don't ever remember my father saying those words. This is obviously a big deal for him. I give a resigned nod and step out of his room to prepare for the ordeal ahead.

⁘ ⁘ ⁘

The next day, I head to the TS office at the Mumbai Business Centre. They moved to a new flashy building recently, to be closer to the new-generation businesses. These days, TS handles a large set of money-laundering and data-theft cases, which is my forte. Unlike this hellish homecoming gift my father has handed me. I am greeted by Roopa, my father's personal secretary, who hands me my coffee, just the way I like it.

I am quite fussy about caffeine, and I become cranky if my morning coffee is not made to my liking. The coffee machine in my house is one of the best gifts my wife ever got for me. That, and she also figured out my favourite coffee blend. Organic Columbian. Dark roast. Coarse ground. Steaming hot. Lots of foam. No sugar. There are theories linking coffee choices to psychological profiles. I remember reading some article about how people who prefer black coffee tend to be psychopaths. I am sure they would have something to say about my caffeine choices as well, but I don't care.

Roopa is one hell of a woman—efficient, punctual and all-knowing—and I am glad she agreed to work with me after my father stepped down because of his poor health. I have always believed in knowing my team well, so I ask Roopa about Sanjay. Sanjay is almost my age, not married and hails from a family of lawyers. Very hardworking and very driven, he is the youngest senior lawyer in the firm and very reputed in his domain. He joined the firm about five years ago and has since worked with Sarvesh on criminal cases. His last case received the Anand Chandra Award, a prestigious accolade in our circles. No wonder my father likes him.

Roopa leads me to the conference room, where Sanjay is waiting for me with a bunch of case files. He has brilliance and confidence written all over his face. As we shake hands and take our seats, I realize that although technically I am his boss, he is far more equipped to deal with this case than I am. I am yet to discover what I bring to the table. I know I will do a damn good job, but I don't know if that will be good enough. In our profession, especially in India, the system is extremely hierarchical. So despite being the boss on paper, I decide we should work as partners. I will need all the help I can get to solve this case.

Sanjay explains the case facts to me as I take down a few notes. The accused, Vishal Mehta, is a twenty-one-year-old final-year engineering student at College of Engineering and Technology, Trombay. The victim is Nitya Harde, a nineteen-year-old second-year student at the same college. Hailing from the residential community close to the college, Nitya was the daughter of a deceased employee at the Trombay power plant. Charges against the accused are sexual abuse and murder. The crime took place in Intox Club, near the college, during the farewell party for graduating students. The victim was found dead in the office room on the first floor of the club at 11:35 p.m. on the 5th of February. She was stabbed with scissors and her carotid artery was cut off. The crime was discovered when Vishal called up the bar owner from the intercom and screamed for help. When the bar owner and his workers rushed upstairs, Vishal was clutching the body of the girl and sobbing. He was immediately taken into police custody. The girl was rushed to the hospital, where she was declared dead on arrival. The post-mortem report stated that the victim died from severe blood loss. There was also evidence of physical abuse and it is suspected that the victim was sexually violated prior to her death. The police found evidence of intercourse, and the victim's jeans were unbuttoned and pulled down to her waist The narrative around the case, as it is now, is this: Vishal forced the girl when she refused to have sex with him, and ended up stabbing her.

However, the accused claims otherwise. According to Vishal, he had consensual and protected sex with Nitya and then went to the bathroom to clean up. When he stepped out of the bathroom, he found his lover lying on the sofa, blood gushing from her neck.

An earlier bail plea made by Mehta's family lawyer was summarily rejected by the Mumbai High Court. The public prosecutor argued that the accused comes from a wealthy and influential family and letting him out on bail will allow him to influence the case in his favour. Public outrage at the heinous crime put pressure on the High Court to put the case on the fast-track list, which allows a maximum of forty-five days from the date of the first hearing to the final verdict.

'The first hearing took place last week, and the next hearing is scheduled for Monday next week. This leaves us just about five working days to prepare our case,' Sanjay concludes.

As I listen to the case facts, I feel a heady mix of terror and sympathy at the monstrosity of the crime. I am immediately hit by a pang of regret at my decision to take up this case. The victim was a young college girl … my mind automatically drifts to my daughter, and I shudder at the unwelcome thought. I quickly push these unsettling thoughts away and focus on the case at hand.

"The girl was not a minor," I note.

Sanjay nods. "That's right. She celebrated her nineteenth birthday two weeks before her death."

I frown and probe further. "Did the two know each other?"

"Yes. They were dating, but we need to get the details."

"And … protected sex? Isn't that odd? Sexual assault is often impulsive, isn't it?"

"Most often than not, yes. But the argument here is that he came to the bar with the deed in mind."

"Hmm... And why does the son of a Bollywood icon study engineering in an Indian college?"

"Mehta is an old fashioned guy. He wanted his son to have a good education before taking up an acting career. CETT is a private college, owned by the Trombay Power Company, which is in turn owned by Mehta's wife's family. It is likely that Vishal got easy admission. We only got the case last Friday. I have obtained some information from a phone call with Kishore Mehta, but that's about it. We were waiting for you before proceeding."

"I understand. I appreciate that you have done the groundwork with all these details. Let's go meet the client today. By the way, do we know anyone on this case?" Relationships are critical in this profession, so I am always looking for leverage.

Sanjay seems a bit surprised by my question. "Need to find out. The DCP may be known to your father."

⁘ ⁘ ⁘

On our way to the Mehtas household, Sanjay takes me through the developments in India's sexual assault laws and what we can expect in court in the following weeks. As we wait for Kishore Mehta to join us in his home office, a middle-aged woman—grief-stricken yet beautiful—takes the chair opposite to us. She is Ratna Mehta, Kishore Mehta's wife.

"My husband will join us shortly. In the meanwhile, I wanted to talk to you about the case."

"Mrs. Mehta, we have just about started working on the case," Sanjay says.

She ignores Sanjay, looks at me and continues. "My son is a gentle soul, Mr. Bhargav. He would never do such a heinous thing. He loved the girl dearly. Please get him out of this mess. The idea that Vishal could kill someone is absurd!"

"Mrs. Mehta, the evidence against your son is very strong," I reply. "But we will do our best. The more information you give us concerning the case, the more it will help us. You mentioned your son was in love with the girl. How long were they seeing each other?"

"For nearly two years. My son even wanted me to talk to my

husband about their relationship. But they broke up towards the end of his third year at college and did not speak or have any contact after that. A few weeks before this incident, he asked me if he could invite Nitya to the farewell party he was planning for his friends at our home. I told him I would think about it."

"So," I ask, "they broke up sometime during the third year and got back together a few weeks before the incident?"

"I am not really sure if they got back or if he was just trying to be friendly and smooth things over."

"Why exactly did they break up Mrs. Mehta?" Sanjay chimes in.

"I am not sure. The two were from very different worlds, in terms of lifestyle and social circles. Perhaps that was the reason."

"Hmm." Sanjay nods. Then, he says, "You said your son is a gentle soul. What did you mean?"

We are both dissecting every word she says to get hold of anything at all that could be useful to the case.

"My son is always kind to the maids and workers at our house. He would never yell at them or even scold them, when they messed up. He would give chocolates to the maids' kids when they bring them home occasionally."

I want to believe her. But I know from experience that at Vishal's age, parents barely know their children all that well. Youth are highly unpredictable and try to hide their impulsive tendencies from their parents.

As we are talking, Kishore Mehta joins his wife. The actor looks well-built and strikingly handsome even at this age.

"Thank you for agreeing to take this case, gentlemen. And Mr. Bhargav, I could not be more grateful to your father for this favour."

"No problem, Sir. We appreciate your faith in us. And please call me Ajay."

Kishore Mehta had signed us on this case on a fixed-fee basis. We are an expensive firm, and this case is going to make a small dent in his pocket. But he never insisted on a success-fee arrangement. In a way, that burdens us even more to not fail him.

He worriedly asks us, "The evidence is bad, isn't it? What are the chances of Vishal getting acquitted?"

"I cannot say, Mr. Mehta. But our first priority is to make a bail plea and get him out on bail."

"Our family lawyer could not convince the judge. The public prosecutor is a tough nut to crack. What is your plan for the next hearing?"

Sanjay briefed me about the public prosecutor on our drive here. The judge respects her a lot, and she has a record of ensuring severe penalties and life sentences against perpetrators in sexual-abuse cases. Apparently, she is notorious for ripping apart the accused with one hell of a cross-examination. Most often than not, people succumb to her verbal onslaught and admit to the offence in a matter of a few questions.

"We need to meet Vishal first, Sir. We will chalk out a plan after speaking to him."

"Please feel free to contact me at any time of the day for any help you want. I want my son out of this mess as quickly as possible. And Ajay, you may have to make a statement to the press."

"What?"

"You see, I am a public figure. So I have a certain responsibility to the press and the public in general. I have an image to uphold.

We haven't addressed people directly until now, and if we delay any further, there may be severe backlash. Things have been getting worse for a while. You must have heard of the Nari Shakti group. They are chasing this case like vultures. Hundreds of people get killed in this country every day and none of those incidents make it even to the corners of the cheapest newspapers. But one transgression by a celebrity, and it makes the primetime headlines for weeks. But don't worry, we have a plan in place, and it's not as bad as you think."

I cringe at his callous description of the incident, but before I can react to whatever he is saying, a petite but confident-looking man strolls in and offers his hand to me. I reciprocate in a bit of a daze.

"This is Nanda, my PR man. He will guide you through our media-management plan. Now, if you will excuse me, gentlemen, I have some business to attend to. Thank you again for your services."

Nanda places some files in front of me and quickly gives me a lowdown. "Mr. Bhargav, as Vishal's principal advocate on this case, you are required to exercise high circumspection while interfacing with the media. Any communication whether direct or indirect, oral or written, to the press and public in general, including social media, cannot be made without our prior approval. We will monitor your interactions closely, and in case your interaction presents any risk to the Mehta's reputation, we will approach you for remedial action, which you must undertake immediately. Please note that it's not just Kishore Mehta. Mrs. Mehta is also a public figure, being one of the key shareholders of the publicly listed Ahuja Industries. After the issues we faced with the family lawyer, we are being extra cautious and would request that our engagement contract be amended to reflect this understanding."

This guy sounds like a taskmaster, and I am impressed with his professionalism and preparation. But something bothers me. "Why was the family lawyer removed?"

At this, Nanda takes the seat adjacent to us and stares at me for a couple of minutes, before responding. "Hmm … After the earlier bail plea was rejected, the lawyer made some unsavoury remarks in front of Vishal and he … he punched him. It was not working out, and the Mehtas decided to replace him."

"Vishal punched the lawyer?" I mutter in a shocked whisper.

But Nanda seems unfazed. "That's in the past. The folders here contain the revised terms, and I would request you to accept them at the earliest. Thank you, gentlemen."

With that, he steps out, leaving Sanjay and me in the room.

Media? What the heck am I going to tell the media? Sure, I have spoken at many conferences and offered my expert opinion to newspapers and journals, but this is a really big deal. Exposure to media would mean a high-focus flashlight on my every move and limelight that may suffocate and destroy my career. I can feel this case consuming me like a python that wraps itself around its prey and crushes its bones before consuming it altogether.

My thoughts are interrupted when Sanjay speaks. "His mother claims he is a gentle soul."

"Mothers are the poorest judges of their sons' characters."

"I will take care of the paperwork. Not to worry."

"Listen Sanjay. Don't get me wrong but I think you must play the role of an advisor on this case. This is a big risk to our careers and reputation."

He nods understandingly and leaves after we agree to meet up with Vishal the next day.

Back in my car, I put on some music. The intense thumping beats of *Haunted* by Beyonce fill my car; they resonates too much with my sullen gloomy feelings, so I switch them off immediately. I take stock of my situation. I am going to defend a guy who may have actually killed this girl, in my very first criminal case in India, and my father owes this family. To top it all, the ruthless media is looking at every opportunity to use my own words against me. If I fail this case, forget India, I don't think I can practise law anywhere. Maybe we will have to move to some low-key country like Cyprus or Bahamas. Thankfully, my wife and I are in some of the most wanted professions, because there is no corner in this world that is devoid of outlaws or patients. I do want to go to the Bahamas, but on a vacation—not like this. I don't give up so easily, so I decide to fight tooth and nail to get this guy out.

At night, I speak to Tavishi and explain my predicament. She offers to set up the house and ensure that we are all ready to move in. "Focus on the case," she says. Tavi is a deadly combination of wit, worldly knowledge and street smartness. Had she not studied medicine, she would have done exceedingly well as a businesswoman or a diplomat.

A smile forms on my lips, as I think about my family. I miss them and need them all the more now.

CHAPTER 3

Vishal

I wake up early in the morning after a disturbed sleep and a bone-chilling nightmare. I dreamt that I was being hanged. It felt so real! I swear I even felt the rope tightening around my neck. I woke up clutching my neck in desperation and kicking my legs. Life in prison is terrifying, and I cannot even drown myself in alcohol to numb this terror.

Oh God! What the fuck is happening to me?

I freshen up a bit, and I'm taken to the visitors' room, where my new lawyers are waiting to speak to me. After my earlier bail plea was rejected and he made some lousy remarks, I punched the douchebag of a family lawyer and now, I have become quite notorious. My father moved heaven and earth to find a new lawyer but in vain. Out of time and options, he called in a favour from his old friend who agreed to take up my case. I am hoping the new guy will get me the hell out of here.

Two guys in their mid-thirties wearing expensive suits and crisp white shirts are seated in the chairs facing the table. They get up as I walk in, and we shake hands. The guy wearing glasses addresses me.

"Hi, Vishal. I am Sanjay Narang, and this is Ajay Bhargav. He is the lead attorney on this case. How are you doing?"

Ajay Bhargav looks super polished with his firm handshake and a confident authoritative demeanour. He is lean, tall and muscular with sharp features, a fair complexion and curious eyes. He looks like a suave businessman or a middle-aged model—nothing like a criminal lawyer who gets his hands dirty. He withdraws his hand after the handshake and inserts both his palms in the pockets of his trousers, waiting for me to respond. His brows are furrowed as he assesses me.

How are you doing? Is he fucking kidding me? After that terrorizing nightmare, I am feeling extremely snarky, so I give it to them. "They served me two slices of stale bread with half a teaspoon of jam in an aluminium plate for breakfast today. Yeah, I am feeling pretty good."

Last night, the guards my mother had bribed were off duty, substituted by an old man who didn't give a rat's ass about my father's celebrity status. Or maybe he was just a smartass who thought he could cut a better deal with mother dearest, if he only lets me taste a piece of this heaven.

Ajay cranes his neck and raises an eyebrow as he stares at me. His face says: *And who do you think is responsible for that delectable meal?* I stare right back at him until he clears his throat and speaks. "Vishal, we want to push your bail petition again in the coming hearing. We would like to go through the case details and other related information with you. We strongly recommend that you tell us every little detail pertaining to this case."

"Where do I begin?"

"Where it all began."

And just like that, I am flooded with memories of the past two years.

❖ ❖ ❖

I had volunteered for a mandatory firefighter training at college, and it was the last day of demonstration to first-year students. A month ago, there was a minor fire accident in our chemistry lab and the fire alarm malfunctioned. Thankfully, the fire was not big enough to injure anyone, but to prepare for the worst, the college had hired a fire protection squad to train a few students, who could act as volunteers in case of any emergency. I had enrolled in a couple of humanitarian courses and practical projects, as they earn us more credits. Since I had just about average grades, these projects were a saving grace.

Since I'm the son of a world-famous Bollywood star, everyone expects me to pursue education abroad and learn arts and theatre to follow in my father's footsteps. But I have always been sort of indifferent to my education and career choices. I am not bad in the good looks department, considering the female fan club I have managed to create over the years. I have inherited my father's height and his voice and diction, with that low authoritative baritone. I have also been blessed with my mother's kind and friendly smile. But since my father is old school, he insisted that I get my basic education in this country, in a college here in Mumbai. After, that, I am free to pursue any career I want. Normally, the people in our circles take up commerce or arts courses. I would have done the same, if not for my overprotective mother who insisted I study engineering at her family college, CETT. I did not score well in any of the competitive exams, so this was an easier way out. CETT is a private college owned by the Ahuja family. It has students from all walks of life and a few of them live at the Trombay Housing Colony near the college. All my friends were rich and famous. Kay, one of my close friends, is the daughter of a local politician. She was attracted to me, I think, because she would tag along for any project I picked up or any course I studied.

That day, Kay and I, along with four other volunteers, were going to demonstrate basic and emergency fire rescue techniques to the freshmen students. We were dressed in white and red t-shirts and were waiting in the lecture hall for all the students to assemble. We started the session and quickly went over the basic rules and then picked up the fire extinguishers for a quick demonstration. After I showed them how to operate, I called for a couple of volunteers for a trial. Two guys came forward and quickly showed the group how to operate the cylinders. Kay then asked a few girls to volunteer. There was silence for a while, and then a small hand went up at the back. She slowly came into view and my head swam at the sight of the most beautiful girl I had ever seen.

The girl looked at me and gently said, "I would like to try. Can you show me how?"

I blinked a couple of times, swooning at the sweetness of her voice, and then proceeded to show her the nozzle operation. She initially struggled with handling the heavy cylinder and almost swayed, but I held her arm firmly. Electricity buzzed through my fingers at that touch, and I took a step back. After a few attempts, she got it right and everybody gave her a round of applause. I presented her a wrist band as a token of appreciation. Then, I asked her name so I could congratulate her.

Nitya - A beautiful name for a beautiful girl.

I shook her hand and felt the electricity pulse through me again. But I had to focus on the task at hand and finish the rest of the demo.

From that day on, I was consumed by thoughts of Nitya. Wanting to know more about her, I talked to Kay. She clearly did not like my interest in Nitya, so she brushed it off. She told me Nitya was some random girl from across the street and that boys like me should not get any ideas about girls like her. She had a point and so, over the next few weeks, I tried my best not to dwell on her.

A few weeks later, I was at the library. It was almost eight in the night and I was browsing for a good book on machine learning. I spotted a closed cabinet labelled "New Books" and found a promising one. After I took the book, I tried to close the door back, but it did not budge. So I applied a little pressure taking support with my left hand on the rack shelf. Suddenly, the door fell forward with a thud and landed on my fingers. I let out a loud yelp and quickly reopened the door, pulling out my injured hand.

"Oh God! What happened? Are you all right? Let me see your fingers."

The voice sounded familiar and I looked up to see Nitya, carefully taking my injured hand into both her palms and examining the wound. My fingers were badly bruised with a deep scar on one of them. My palm had swollen slightly and it hurt like hell.

"I don't think they are fractured, but they do need immediate attention. Come on, let's go to the lab; there might be some ointment or pill you could use."

Honestly, the pain was not that bad now. But I was enjoying her company, so I played along and let her take me to the lab. The whole lab was empty, and we looked around for a while until we finally found the first-aid box. Nitya grabbed some gel and applied it on my knuckles. Then she handed me a paracetamol pill.

"Are you going home on a bike? Will you be able to ride it?"

I drove a car but could not have driven with those injured fingers, so I made a call to my driver to pick me up. It would take almost an hour for him to come over, so I got an idea. "Someone will pick me in an hour. Why don't we go and grab some dinner?"

"Hmm. It's quite late, and I need to get home. We may have a surprise test tomorrow."

"We could just go to the college canteen. I am really hungry and none of my friends is around, so ... please?

She agreed, and we both headed over to the canteen. Each of us ordered a plate of cheese Maggi and a glass of orange juice. I paid for both of us—a measly hundred bucks. As we sat eating, I looked at her face, committing each feature to memory—her perfect lips and luscious curly hair.

"We met the other day at the fire demonstration. Do you remember?"

Oh! How could I not remember? But I put up a facade.

"Uh, I guess. Which stream?"

"Computer Science. First year. How about you?"

"The same. But third year."

"Hey! I forgot to ask. What's your name? I don't remember from that day."

"Vishal."

"I am Nitya."

"That's a nice name. By the way, this cheese Maggi is delicious. I can't believe it's just twenty-five bucks." The yummy plate was cheaper than the Granola bar I had in the morning for breakfast.

"You should try the fried version too. It's really yummy. So, where do you live?"

Either she really did not know who I was, or she was feigning ignorance. I knew I was quite famous on campus.

"I live near the Mumbai Club. How about you? Where are you from?"

"I live in the Trombay Housing Colony. My father was an

employee at the power plant. He passed away a few years ago. But we still own a house there.”

“Oh, I am so sorry about your father. So, do you have any siblings?”

“Yes. A brother. He graduated from this college last year. Now he works for a manufacturing company in the city. His name is Niraj. Do you happen to know him?”

“Not really. We may not have met often. So, how do you like our college?”

“It’s a great place. A lot of people from our colony are here. So it’s all familiar. I am very comfortable now. I heard we had 100 percent placements this year. That’s a really good thing.”

“Yeah, I know. What do you do in your free time?”

“Nothing exciting. I am a very boring person. I just like to read and sing.”

“You sing? What kind of music?”

“I learnt classical music. But I sing all sorts of songs. I like fast beat songs like rap and rock music.”

“That’s great. I play the guitar. I am the lead guitarist in Souffle, our college music band.”

“Wow! That’s amazing. I would love to sing to a big audience someday.”

“I think you should meet the rest of our band and audition. If you fit in well, you will surely get a lot of opportunities for big performances.”

“Sure, I would love that.”

"Give me your phone number and I will text you when we assemble next time."

We exchanged our numbers, and I offered to drop her back home. She politely refused, so I walked her to the bus stop. I felt strangely rejuvenated after the conversation and I could not help the splitting grin I had on my face on the drive back home.

CHAPTER 4

Vishal

I chanced upon Nitya, the next time, after a guest lecture that was attended by all the computer science students. She tried to avoid me, but I steered her away from the crowd.

"Hey! What's wrong?"

"Well, you and me. We are from two different planets. I don't think this is a good idea."

"What? We are just being friends. Nothing more." I was not sure if I was trying to convince me or herself.

"Okay …" She sounded unsure and uncomfortable, so I tried to distract her with something exciting.

"Hey, listen, Souffle is meeting tonight to plan an event. Do you want to join? I will text you the location once it's finalized."

"Sure. That's very nice of you!"

That night, we met at the Souffle gathering near the fountain at the entrance of our college. I wanted to text her so badly and talk to her, but I did not want to come across as clingy. Souffle was planning a performance for College Day, and we were shortlisting songs for the concert. We were looking for another female singer in our band and decided to try out Nitya's voice. She sang a soft Indian melody, *Raabta*, and all of us were impressed by her sweet voice and impressive range. She quickly got comfortable talking to the band members and was very inquisitive about the various genres in music.

Over the next few weeks, Nitya and I became good friends. Kay constantly criticized my friendship with Nitya and tried to demean her at every chance she got. When I couldn't stand her nagging any more, I started avoiding Kay and instead spent more time with Nitya. One day, I invited her to my home for practice. She was hesitant at first but agreed after much convincing. Some of her friends would jump at the chance to meet my father and get a selfie or an autograph or even take a peek into our flamboyant lives. But Nitya hardly showed any interest or excitement. In the time I spent with her, she never asked me to buy a thing. She would even pay for the ice cream we occasionally bought at the bakery near our college.

So that day, when she came home for our practice session, my mother was around. I introduced the two of them, and they had a polite conversation about music. But after she left, I had a tough conversation with my mother

"Vishal, I understand she is your friend, but please don't take it any further."

"Mom! What do you mean? I am not a child, and I don't like you dictating my life like this."

"I am NOT dictating your life! You of all people should not use such words with me! I am only cautioning you against something foolish you might do. You father will go crazy if he knows about your 'friendship' with this girl."

"Okay, Mom. Thanks for your advice but let me be."

I knew my mother always watched out for me, so I tried to convince myself that this was just friendship. It was not like either of us had expressed any affection towards each other. I suppressed my feelings and sentiments and went about my life as usual.

Our performance during the college concert was a stupendous success. The band received rousing applause for its rendition of the song *Maa Tujhe Salam.* In addition to the patriotic song, we chose a medley of sorts—*Campus* by Vampire Weekend and *Now We Are Free*, OST from the Gladiator. Nitya did not get too much airtime, except for a small piece of the lilt in the OST. But her voice was so captivating, everyone was awestruck by her performance. Given her lack of exposure to international music, I never guessed she would be able to sing the idioglossia so well. After the concert, our band decided to celebrate the victory with a booze party. Nitya was hesitant to join, so in lieu of the party, I offered to take her to dinner the next day. Again, she refused, so we decided to head to our regular ice-cream parlour to grab our mutual favourite "apple pie sundae". It was a beautiful early evening, and we decided to take a walk along the beach nearby.

When she started to hum some classical melody, I felt this unstoppable urge to kiss her. I held her face in my palms and angled my head to press my lips softly to hers. For a minute, she was lost in the kiss, but then she pulled back abruptly, pushing me in the process.

"No!"

I blinked a couple of times.

"We cannot do this! Vishal, please, let's not complicate this."

"Hey! There is nothing wrong about giving in to your feelings. Don't tell me you don't feel this attraction between us."

She stared at me for a couple of minutes. "I feel it. But I don't want to act on it or take it any further. Vishal, you are the son of a celebrity. You are wealthy, sophisticated and you lead a high-end lifestyle. I am just a middle-class girl from around the corner. My life is simple. I am not the dating kind. I am not girlfriend material. So please, let's just be friends."

"Nitya, I am rich but that doesn't mean I am not allowed to have feelings. I really like you, and I want to spend as much time as possible with you. I feel excited and happy when I am around you. I cannot ignore my feelings and act as if there is nothing between us. We are not doing anything wrong. We are just admitting what we mean to each other."

"I don't want to argue about this. And I am sure you will soon realize all this is temporary infatuation. It will pass."

"Not if we don't let it."

"It's either friends or nothing," she declared.

I did not want to lose her. I knew that would be too much to handle. I wanted to have a piece of her always, no matter how small it was and in whatever way she allowed. And so, I acquiesced.

"Okay. I promise I won't bring this up again. But let's not end our friendship. I am sorry I crossed the line. Let's just forget what happened and go back to being friends."

She nodded in understanding, and we walked to her bus stop, discussing some inconsequential stuff.

⊹ ⊹ ⊹

Over the next few days, it became very apparent that Nitya was trying to not be alone with me. We only met for Souffle meetings. Her attitude was civil, but she was surely holding herself back. I really missed our earlier comfortable equation. This new forced distance was killing me. Kay somehow figured out my situation with Nitya and grabbed the opportunity to make a move on me. She was a constant visitor at my home and even expressed a never-there-before interest in my mother's new passion for baking. My friend, Sameer, the son of a top Indian music director and a key member of our band, had feelings for Kay. But she had her eyes set on me as I came from a wealthier and more influential family. I watched their interactions with amusement and felt sorry for Sameer. I tried to convince him to move on and find love elsewhere, but he was adamant about winning Kay's affections. Life just about went on like this for a while.

A few weeks later, I got an opportunity to work for my uncle, who was the head of operations and IT at the power plant. They were setting up a new control system, and he suggested I work with their IT team for a couple of hours after college, a few days in the week. Everything at that place was new to me, and it was an effective distraction from my feelings for Nitya.

One evening, as I was walking towards my car parked at the end of the road, I heard a low growl coming from one of the alleys near the office. I saw a hound-like dog with its mouth open and tongue hanging out, ready to pounce on a girl. The girl's back was to me, and her duffel bag was hung low from her trembling hands. I immediately recognized the duffel bag.

As I walked towards her, I realized Nitya was so terrified by the beast in front of her that she could not even acknowledge my presence. There was a look of utter horror on her face, and tears were streaming down her fair cheeks. My heart went out to her and I stepped in.

When I was a kid, my grandfather got me a terrier puppy as a birthday gift. Being an only child, I always craved company at home, and this puppy was such a happy companion. The poor thing passed away when I started college. Having had a dog for so long, I was very familiar with the canine species. I recalled all the tricks I knew, moved closer to the dog, and slowly extended my palm to give it a rub under its neck saying soft soothing words to calm it down.

"Is there any food in your bag?" I asked Nitya.

She gave a weak nod and hastily passed the duffel bag to me. I opened it to find a chicken sandwich—the cause of this whole mess. I quickly threw the packet far away from Nitya, and the dog rushed to grab the goodies. Nitya let out a huge sigh and tears started rolling down her face. My heart went out to her, and I put a reassuring arm around her.

To my utter surprise, she immediately grabbed me, wrapping her arms around me in a tight embrace, her head pressed against my chest. This sudden display of emotion made me freeze on the spot. She looked up at me, and before I could realize what was happening, we were locked in a passionate kiss.

I was the first to break away. "Hey! It's okay. It's just a dog, Nitya. He smelled the sandwich and wanted that."

"I am terribly scared of dogs. When he cornered me, I didn't know what to do. Thank you for saving me, Vishal."

"Well, when you put it like that ... you're welcome. Besides, you've already returned the favour many times over."

She gave me a shy smile. "I do like you. So much."

"I like you too. More than you will ever know. Come on, let me drop you home."

We walked back towards the car, holding hands, smiles beaming on our faces. It was clear that she had overcome whatever reservations she had about our relationship. As we parted ways for the night, I gave her a soft kiss and wished her goodnight. That night, I tossed and turned in the bed, too excited to sleep. I had been physically intimate with many girls before—much more than kissing. But this kiss seemed special, as if it were my first kiss ever.

The next few weeks were pure bliss. We hung out a lot, and we showed affection towards each other in abundance and without any inhibitions. Nitya was still hesitant to accept any expensive gifts from me, even though I wanted to spend all my monthly allowance on buying her things. The only exception she made was the Bose earphones I gave her, but she kept clarifying they were "on loan" and that she would return them to me whenever she could afford new ones.

During spring, Nitya's brother, Niraj, was out of town for a company off-site and her mother had gone on a pilgrimage trip. We grabbed the opportunity to freely go around town, with no fear of getting caught. We went bowling in an upscale mall. She fared miserably but looked at me with such pride when I got a few good shots. We watched a lot of movies together. We composed silly tunes and sang some ridiculous lines.

Life was good but something was still missing. While I was happy with Nitya, I wanted to take our relationship to the next level. My nights were filled with wet dreams and days were spent stealing opportunities to get as close to her as I could. She was still underage, so I had to hold myself back. Every night, I took a cold shower to block out my dirty fantasies. Her eighteenth birthday was in a few weeks, and I was busy making grand romantic plans, which would set into motion the chain of events that would eventually lead to my downfall.

CHAPTER 5

Vishal

I wanted to take my girlfriend on a romantic date, complete with some melodious music and a candle-light dinner. But it was not possible to get that kind of time; our final exams were in a few weeks, so both of us had a lot of preparation to do.

While I was desperate for deeper physical intimacy with Nitya, I knew it would take a hell of a time to convince her to take that kind of chance with me. Nitya came from a very conservative family, where it was a real big deal for a girl to have a physical relationship before marriage. Her family belonged to a religious group that met every week, and Nitya told me that she got interested in music by singing devotional songs for weekly congregations. So, I had to make her trust me, that we were both in this for the long haul. My parents were planning to go on a vacation soon after my final exams, and I would have the house to myself. I planned to use that time effectively. My father was trying to send me to London to learn theatre, but I thought I could use my newfound interest in the powerplant IT to stay back and spend time with Nitya instead. I was not sure if my father would buy my pathetic excuse, but a guy could hope.

The previous week, during one of our rendezvous moments in the college storeroom, as I nuzzled her neck, I had inhaled a sweet and intoxicating combination of vanilla and melon and that made me want to sink my teeth into her sweet skin. When I asked her, she told me a distant relative of theirs from the States had to come to visit them and got her some body wash. She said she really loved it. So, for her birthday, I decided to get her a basket of skin products.

One of my friends, Yogi, had told me about the storeroom. He and his girlfriend would frequently go there for their romantic escapades. This room had become my favourite place in the whole world—even with its dim lights; stacks of papers; inches thick dust layers on every surface; the stench of oil, old books and cement; and the annoying dampness and eerie vibe.

We were both entangled in a passionate embrace, Nitya raking her fingers through my hair as I explored her petite body with my hands.

"Oh God, I can't wait to make you mine!"

"You always have dirty thoughts on your mind!"

'Wrong. I am always thinking of you."

"Let's just enjoy this right now."

"Sure. Except I don't know how much control I have. I want you so badly!"

She looked into my eyes with a mischievous gleam.

"Maybe I should put some distance between us to ease your misery."

"Or you can put me out of my misery altogether."

"Vishal ..."

"Shhh ... I know baby. But there are lots of other things that we can do. Please, just let me show you what mind-numbing pleasure is. Trust me, you won't regret your decision."

She frowned. "How do you know so much?"

I was about to respond when I heard a loud bang. I looked up and saw Niraj standing behind Nitya, on the verge of breaking something. He had already rammed into the door and broken the latch open to get in. The look on his face was deadly and bone-chilling, and Nitya automatically moved in front of me in a protective stance. I stepped forward, swallowed the dread, and called out to him.

"Niraj ..."

He abruptly raised his palm in a warning gesture and turned to his sister. "Nitya, come here!"

"Niraj, please don't harm Vishal."

He silenced her protests with a single look and addressed me. "I am giving you this one opportunity to leave before you corrupt my sister anymore. Forget about her and never try to contact her again. If you ever do, I will destroy you. You may have power and influence. But you also have a reputation and standing in society, and that is exactly the weapon I am going to use against you. I am sure it will cost your father dearly, and he is not going to like it. In this war, he will surely side with me."

Before I could respond, he grabbed Nitya by her hand and left. Nitya did not even turn to look at me as she left me and my heart in pieces.

Later that night, I received a text from Nitya telling me how sorry she was and how she really wanted us to be together. But she could not go against her family, so she was breaking up with me. She insisted that I shouldn't try to contact her or convince her in any way.

I was devastated. It felt as though someone had stabbed me right in my chest and twisted the damn knife. The agony was unbearable. That day, I realized the depth of my feelings for her. I loved her. I *really* loved her. And I was not sure how to deal with her loss.

After we were discovered, Niraj asked to speak to my father, having taken the contact details from the principal. He told my father everything and requested him to intervene if I ever contacted his sister. My father was only too happy to oblige. He gave me an earful that day and made me promise not to pursue a commoner like Nitya. He was happy that she broke things off and was pleasantly surprised that they were not gold-diggers trying to make a quick buck from this whole affair.

The next few weeks, I was barely alive. I was angry at everything and everyone. Nitya, for not fighting for us; her brother, for discovering us; this society, for its stupid boundaries and restrictions; my parents, for feeling relieved at my loss; and most of all myself, for allowing this to happen in the first place. Nitya severed all connections with me and even stopped coming for the monthly Souffle meets. My band members knew what had happened, and they were more than understanding—although this whole issue also meant the loss of a very valuable singer. Sameer still requested her to sing the national anthem as a solo on the convocation day as an exception, because we could not get a replacement. That did not require her to interact with me, so she agreed. As expected, her performance was exceedingly wonderful.

My music now lacked passion, and I too stopped playing for the band. The guitar held some painful memories, so I avoided it with vengeance. I quickly became unbearable at home. Everybody feared my mood swings, and the servants just did their job and hastily walked out of my room. My mother kept our conversations to a minimum.

I somehow managed to scrape through my final exams, and on the day of the last exam, I partied with my friends the whole night and drank myself to a stupor. The next morning, I woke up sprawled out on my bed, with a terrible headache. My mother entered the room and handed me a glass of water and some pills. She had a worried, panicked look on her face that forebode some very bad things for me.

"Vishal, your father wants to talk to you. He is waiting for you downstairs."

"Oh God, Mom! Do I at least get a few minutes to freshen up?"

"Don't worry, whatever your father says will be a wake-up call in itself."

"Mom, what happened?"

"You don't remember?"

"No."

"Vishal! What's wrong with you? You are letting a nobody of a girl destroy your entire career and life?"

"Mom! What the hell happened?"

"You got into a fight with Akshay and beat him up. Badly. You should thank your father. He spoke to Akshay's Dad and convinced him to not press charges."

"What? Mom – really? I don't remember a thing."

It was then that I registered my bruised knuckles and a looming ache in my ribs. It must have been a big fight. I tried to remember what exactly had caused me to become so violent. I remembered him calling Nitya a whore, but I couldn't get myself to recollect the whole incident. I knew I was in deep trouble. I quickly freshened up and headed downstairs to face my father. As I took the last step, he turned around and icily greeted me. "Good morning, my dear prince."

"Dad, please …"

"Not a word from you! You don't have to say anything. Whatever you did is more than enough. Shame on you! I can't believe you have become a lovesick fool. Do you even know the consequences of your reckless actions? He could have pressed charges, and you would be rotting in prison. I had to embarrass myself, apologize to his father, and bring you out of this mess."

"I am sorry, Dad."

"The time for apologies is over, Vishal. You have been nothing but a disappointment to me. You need to get out of here. I have arranged for you to join the Oxford New Arts Society for a two-month course. Your flight is tomorrow. Pack your bags and come back only when your college reopens after the summer break."

"Dad, I am not interested in that course!"

"Okay, fine! Tell me what you want to do next, and we will discuss what to do with your vacation."

I wasn't even sure what to do with the next hour, let alone my career and life. So, I stayed silent and let him make the decisions for me.

"It is decided then. No more discussion on this subject."

I had no choice but to agree to his proposal, and frankly speaking, I hoped it would be an effective distraction from my woes. Unlike what people believed, being the son of a successful man is less of a blessing and more of a curse. Because, no matter what people say, you have this inherent ambition to be as good as your father, if not better. And that ambition is a source of high pressure. People often say that a steady relationship is an anchor. I now understood what they mean. Your life, choices and decisions revolve around that person and having a locus of control is one hell of a comfort. I had lost my anchor. Having tasted the comfort of love, being suddenly deprived of it, I felt like a wanderer in the desert, robbed of the water that he had been drinking.

CHAPTER 6

Vishal

I started my course in London with the intention of sitting in the classroom and waiting for the course to get over just for the sake of it. But slowly, I realized that I enjoyed arts and theatre. In my life till now, movies never actually interested me. Commercial Bollywood films back home were too shallow, and I drowned myself in music to pass the time. I never had a passion for cinema, and the whole paraphernalia that came with it. But a week at the Oxford New Arts Society changed my perspective. In the first week of the course, we were asked to watch the movie *War Horse*, by Steven Spielberg. This was the first serious movie I had ever seen. I only ever knew Spielberg for *Jurassic Park* and *Minority Report*, so this gem of a movie was a pleasant surprise to me. Being an animal lover, I nearly wept at the end of the movie, when Albert and Joey finally reunite after their respective turbulent journeys. In that moment, I understood the power of good cinema. It can take you into a different realm and make you live there, and sometimes, the impressions and emotions are so lasting that they serve as an escape from your regular overbearing thoughts. From that day, I pursued my courses with a newfound vigour and earned my tutor's admiration.

I also became friends with Amrita, the daughter of a South Indian film producer. She wanted to pursue a career in acting and was the only other Indian student at the centre. She was older than me by a year and I liked her carefree attitude towards life. She was so different from the women I had seen all my life. I thought South Indian women were conservative, but she proved me wrong. This girl was a contemporary intellectual who held strong views on most subjects. Even though we had nothing much in common—she did not even speak Hindi well—I was surprised that I actually enjoyed her company.

At the end of the course, we had a small farewell party where I drank without a care in the world. Next morning, to my utter shock, I woke up to find a very naked Amrita sleeping next to me. We both realized we had gotten very drunk and had sex in the hotel room—although neither of us remembered what exactly happened. I was sure she was the more conscious participant between the two of us. She told me that I repeatedly called out the name "Nitya" during my sleep. She understood that I still had some unreciprocated feelings for an ex-girlfriend, so she was happy to remain friends with me and not take our one night stand any further.

After the course, I came back to India and went back to college for my final year. I just wanted the course to get over and really prayed that I didn't come across Nitya, although that seemed unlikely. A few weeks later, Amrita called me saying she had moved to Mumbai for a few auditions, and we got in touch again. I took her around Mumbai, and we had a lot of fun. But we still remained friends. On one of our days out, we participated in a beach-cleaning drive as a part of the "Swachh Bharat Mission". Our efforts gathered a lot of press coverage, and my parents were very happy with the "positive influence" Amrita had on me.

For the annual College Day performance, my band insisted that I join them. Amrita convinced me that I could not run away from my past, that the best way to deal with it was to swallow it like a bitter pill and move on to the next chapter of life. I had a long life ahead, and I needed to take stock of it before I ended up wasting it away. I finally agreed to perform with the band. Sameer told me that Nitya felt the same way, and she had agreed to sing as well. I was totally sceptical about facing her, but to my surprise, we managed quite well, albeit being distant and polite with each other. This time around, Nitya was paired with Yaksh, one of the male singers of the band, so we did not have many opportunities to connect.

As is the tradition with our band, we chose an eclectic medley of songs for the performance and Nitya outdid herself during the rendition of our national anthem, which was a solo female performance. I am sure a couple of music lovers in the audience must have shed a tear or two at the intensity and passion in her voice. She looked jubilant when she received a token of appreciation from our Guest of Honour. Her eyes lit up in happiness, and there was a carefree smile on her face. She seemed completely oblivious to my presence; I was convinced that Nitya had moved on. Our band invited her to the customary celebration party, but she politely declined.

It was an early winter evening. I was walking towards my car when I heard Amrita call out to me. I turned around, and she ran towards me and engulfed me in a tight hug. I was momentarily stunned but she rambled on about her latest audition, and how it went off very well and that she bagged the lead actress role in a Bollywood film. Her excitement was infectious, and I laughed along with her until I heard someone sniffle at a distance. I raised my head over Amrita's shoulders to find Nitya looking at us with an intense emotion. I released Amrita immediately and called out to Nitya. Amrita understood what was going on, and she immediately let go of me so I could take care of the situation.

I ran after Nitya and grabbed her arm, even as she was walking away from me. She feigned indifference at first and gave me a cold shoulder. But I was having none of it, and I led her towards a small coffee shop behind the bus stop. She did not try to stop me, and I took that as a positive sign. We sat on a small bench, and there was an awkward silence between us for some time. Finally, I decided to speak.

"It's not what you think. Amrita is just a good friend."

"Vishal. It's okay. You don't have to explain anything to me. We broke up a long time ago. You have obviously moved on, and now I mean nothing to you. I was just overcome by my own feelings for a minute there, but I am okay now. I am sorry, I did not mean to intrude."

"You will always mean something to me, Nitya. Besides, what made you think I have moved on? It's a very convenient assumption on your part."

"Don't say things like that. I am not the one partying around and hugging a woman in a very public display of affection."

"Oh! So, you have been keeping tabs on me."

"Not intentionally. But when it's right in front of my eyes …"

I sighed because the last thing I wanted was a fight with her. "Amrita is just a friend. But I want to be honest with you. We had sex once in London."

She gasped in shock, so I quickly continued, "But I was stupid drunk, and neither of us really remember what happened or how. I have not so much as thought about another girl since I met you. I don't even have the bandwidth to think about myself. My thoughts are consumed by you. I am barely surviving."

Her eyes turned moist, and I knew she was holding back her tears. But she composed herself and whispered, "I have missed you too. So much."

I thanked the heavens and stars, because that was the most uplifting thing I had heard in a long time. But I needed to seal the deal then and there. "Nitya, it's obvious we still have feelings for each other. But you need to trust me. You cannot give up on us again. You need to trust me to take care of everything, which I damn sure will. You should know by now I am not looking for just a good time with you. I'm in this heart and soul, and you need to be too. Otherwise, it's not going to work, and it's going to destroy both of us."

"I know. I trust you. I promise I will never leave you again." She took my hand in hers and gave it a gentle reassuring squeeze.

❖ ❖ ❖

We were back together, and I couldn't be happier. This time, Nitya did not hold back. She returned my affection with equal enthusiasm, and we resumed our courtship.

We once skipped our respective afternoon classes to have some fun time at the mall. We played a few laser games and a VR challenge and ate dinner at a Mexican eatery. Nitya was completely in love with Mexican food. After our day out, we sat in a garden adjoining the mall, and I asked her if she had any issues about my friendship with Amrita. I did not want to make Nitya insecure, so I had stopped speaking to Amrita after I patched up things with Nitya. Amrita had once dropped a text checking to see if all was well at my end and telling me that she was leaving for Bangalore on a family emergency. But I never returned her text.

"I know you don't have feelings for her, but I am not sure about Amrita."

"Why do you say so?"

"Because some people can be very good at hiding their true feelings."

Her worried and serious tone took me by surprise, so I probed further. "What do you mean? Did something happen when we were apart?"

"No, nothing … I am just cautioning you. You spent a lot of time with her. You even had sex. Maintaining a casual and friendly relationship just sounds undoable."

"We don't remember a thing about that night, Nitya. Maybe I cannot vouch for Amrita. But I am all and only yours."

"That makes me really, really happy." Nitya gave me a shy smile, and we went about the rest of the dinner peacefully.

My graduation was fast approaching, and although Nitya had two more years, I had to leave college in a few months. To be honest, I had not decided what to do with my life after college. The only thing I was sure about was that I had to be in this city and as close to Nitya as possible. I strongly considered working for Trombay Industries, my maternal uncle's firm. Although I knew he would be enthusiastic about having me on board, I was not sure my father would like the plan very much. I knew that even if I took up work there, it would be temporary, and I would have to eventually chalk out my career plan and finalize it as soon as possible. I also knew that Nitya and I could not possibly keep our relationship under wraps for such a long time. It would eventually come out. Although Nitya was more confident about rooting for us this time, we would not be taken seriously. We were too young to make big plans, and I did not know one thing about making a life together. But I felt guilty about hiding our relationship from my mother, and I really wanted her to approve of it. I needed to start with baby steps, so I decided I could ease Nitya into her mind by inviting her over to my house for the farewell party I had planned during early summer.

While there were these pressing concerns that had invaded my mind, I never let them dampen my mood and spoil my time with

Nitya. I wanted to make the best of our time together and enjoy our life to the fullest.

CHAPTER 7

Vishal

It was the most blissful time of my life. My relationship with Nitya was going steadily well. We still met secretly, but she was not as afraid of getting caught as she was earlier. She was confident that we were doing nothing wrong, and I was sure she would stand up for us and fight with her brother if he discovered our renewed relationship. Our physical intimacy had improved as well, and Nitya was eager to take it to the next level. She trusted me to take care of her no matter what.

It was the day of the farewell party. It was customary for students to throw a farewell party a few weeks before our exams, as none of us wanted to party after the results were out and our futures were up in the air. The usual party venue was the bar near our college. It was run by Toby Fernandez, a stout middle-aged guy who had known many batches of the CETT students. Toby took care of the students at the party. He made sure there were no incidents and that everyone left the venue safely. There had not been a single incident at the bar despite the hundreds of college students who frequented the bar and partied into the late hours of the night. I think it gave some comfort to the parents, too, knowing that their kid was at this bar and nowhere else.

That night, Nitya agreed to stay with me till about 11 p.m. She had convinced her mom and brother that she would be at the bar along with her friends and that she would return before midnight. One of her classmates, Mihir, from the same community, had offered to take the girls home after the party. That was the first time that Nitya and I were in a club, and we had planned to do a lot of dancing. I promised myself not to drink too much as I wanted to be in my senses to savour my time with her.

The party started at 9 p.m. Nitya was dressed in a red top with frills, plain jeans and small pencil heels. Even in such a simple outfit, she looked deliciously sexy. She initially danced with her group of her friends, until I moved towards her and slowly steered her to a corner. We danced for some time in tune to the thumping rock music, before the music turned into a slow sensual number—*I Don't Deserve You* by Paul Van Dyck, and then Bryan Kearney and Plumb's *All Over Again*.

I was sure everyone noticed that she had been dancing mostly with me, and we both would have to deal with some suspicions the next day. But I didn't care about the damn consequences and gave in to my desire. Keeping up the dance, with my hips swaying in rhythm, I slowly led her away from the busy crowd and towards the stairs that led to the office-cum-break room on the first floor of the bar. The room was mostly used by Toby to manage the bar business. I knew it had a couch, since I met Toby there a few times. That night, he was busy laughing and dancing with the girls. Once we got inside the room, I made sure to lock the door and not switch on the lights. There was a dim night lamp at the corner, and there was light seeping in through the windows, from the streetlights near the bar. That would suffice for what I had in mind. The door to the room had a rectangular see-through panel, so I drew Nitya towards the couch and away from the office desk.

We started kissing passionately, and oh-so-slowly I placed my hands inside her frill top to touch her curves. Soon, we were making passionate love with each other. I put my hands on her mouth to muffle her screams. We both quickly collapsed with pleasure, and I gave her a lingering kiss on her lips as she lay there, totally dazed and exhausted. I released myself from her embrace to get up and use the washroom.

An important lesson my father taught me when I became an adult was to always make sure to use protection for any intimate escapades, I ever engaged in. He had drilled the message into my head with enough horror stories and anecdotes that I am sure I wouldn't forget the lesson even in my sleep. After Nitya and I reconciled, I made it a point to carry condoms with me whenever we met—you know, just to be safe and sure. So, this time too, I remembered to use protection, and later, flushed it away. After I finished my business, I tried to open the door, only to realize the knob was stuck. I had to fumble with it a couple of times before it finally opened.

I took a step into the room to be greeted by a horrendous sight that I couldn't even imagine in my wildest nightmares. Nitya was lying on the floor in a pool of blood, a pair of scissors sticking out of her throat. I rushed to her side and dropped to my knees. I held her and wept, and soon, I was screaming. But nothing happened. It was then that I realized there was loud music playing downstairs and even an explosion could not be heard over those decibels. I desperately looked around for help and found a landline on the office desk. The receiver kept falling from my sweaty palms as I tried to punch in the number. Finally, I held it firm against my ear and managed to connect to the bartender. He picked up the phone after a few rings, and I screamed for help at the top of my voice.

A few moments later, people rushed in. Everything after that was a blur. I was cuffed and taken into custody by two police officers and deposited in the Trombay Jail. I operated like a robot with barely any awareness of my surroundings. The police clicked a lot of pictures, asked me some questions, to which I barely managed to croak out the answers. Early next day, I saw my mother and that's when I finally broke down and sobbed like a baby. My lover was dead, and I was destroyed for the rest of my life.

My mother explained the situation to me. The FIR had been submitted by the bar owner Toby, and the case has been filed in the Bombay High Court by Nitya's brother. My father and I became the news of the nation in a matter of a few hours. The heinous crime had been broadcasted on every news channel, and the entire nation was overcome with shock, grief and anger over the gruesome murder of an innocent girl. A bit of solace to my father was that he was influential and held a good reputation amongst his circles, so the chief minister and the chief of police tried to keep their statements as neutral as possible without offending anyone's sentiments, at the same time assuring justice to the victim. My father was also able to pull some strings and make my life at the prison slightly easier by giving me small concessions, such as access to a phone and frequent visits from my mother.

But my father himself was furious and was barely able to contain his rage when he met me. He was just short of strangling me himself, and I felt he might as well go through with it to save us both from this hell. He blamed me for a lot of things—getting back with the girl, my drinking, my stupid decision to sleep with Nitya, but most importantly for compromising his reputation and social status. During one of our meetings, he told me that he would have rather preferred I rot in prison for the rest of myself, except that would devastate my mother and leave him without an heir. Normally, I would have answered back, but I was too shocked and confused and only managed an inappropriate giggle. That finally convinced him that I had really gone insane. My mother begged him to go easy on me, insisted that I was innocent. But it all fell on deaf ears. I suspected that my mother was not too convinced of my innocence either. Her faith in me was an outcome of motherly desperation for her only offspring.

Over the next few days, the situation deteriorated. The Nari Shakti group, an NGO that provides legal aid to victims and families of sexual abuse and domestic violence, had approached Niraj and they got Tarakeshwari, a formidable advocate, as the public prosecutor on this case. She was considered an expert on this subject, and she had happily agreed to represent the victim's family.

The reaction at my college was equally sobering. All the college students had started a candle protest demanding expeditious justice for their dear friend and collegemate. Although the college was owned by my mother's family, they were helpless against the angry mob of students and remained silent spectators. Sameer was the only one who visited me in the prison cell. He was truly sorry for what had happened and believed I was innocent, but he was not sure how he could help me. None of my other friends came to visit me. I was surprised that Amrita never visited me either. Maybe she was worried about the effect our friendship could have on her upcoming movie project.

The family lawyer my father sent made a lousy representation of my bail petition and the judge denied my plea without so much as a minute of consideration. Later that day, my lawyer and I had a meeting where he asked me some questions and told me that I needed to be prepared and conditioned before the next hearing. At the end of our meeting, it felt as if he was pretty confident that I had indeed killed Nitya. That I was a privileged, spoilt sexual predator. He suggested that I put the blame on the girl instead and paint her as a gold-digger who seduced and manipulated me. That is when I totally lost it and punched the bastard right on his filthy mouth.

After my family lawyer left the case, my father found it extremely difficult to get a competent replacement to fight my case. Everyone knew the risk involved and how that would affect their reputation. This country had recently seen many cases of wealthy and influential men taking advantage of poor innocent girls and getting away with it by delaying the cases or tampering with the evidence or negotiating a settlement with the victims' families. So, a client like me was a liability to any lawyer. Then, there was the media. Situations such as mine were a delicious feast for the media, and they left no stone unturned to make it as melodramatic and entertaining as possible. Thanks to the media frenzy, any lawyer associated with this case had to face the consequences of defeat and the loss of business that would ensue. It took a while before my father was able to find a new lawyer for me. There was a strange confidence and calm on his face when he told me about the new lawyer, and I was momentarily surprised by my father's hope.

I ease back to the present as my story runs out, facing the two gentlemen who perhaps hold the key to my freedom. Something about this guy Ajay makes me feel better. Maybe it's his calming demeanour or his no-nonsense attitude.

Having told him the entire story, albeit leaving out some intimate details, I look him in the eye and ask,

"Do you believe I am innocent, Mr. Bhargav?"

CHAPTER 8

Ajay

"Do you believe I am innocent, Mr. Bhargav?"

Frankly, I don't know. "Vishal, as I said earlier, we will try our best to get you out on conciliatory bail. That's the first priority. So, I need to gather as much ammunition as possible to make that happen, especially after an earlier failed attempt. And you can call me, Ajay."

"Okay. So, what do you need me to do? Shed a few tears and make it more believable?"

I note the acerbity in his tone but choose to ignore it. "No. But I need some solid ground. You mentioned the college farewell party happened before your exams. So, when are the exams scheduled?"

"The first one starts on 30th March. And then they are spread out over ten days."

"Okay. So how were your grades in college?"

"I do very well in practical assessments. Top three in class. Theory, not so great. Overall, I am just about average."

"By practical assessments, you mean, on a computer in a lab with a specific time limit?"

"Yes."

"Great. So, let me see what we can do. The prosecutor may press for cross-examination of a few witnesses after the bail plea is closed. We'll need to be prepared. I will meet you tomorrow for more questions. Take care till then."

"Thank you."

As we walk out and approach the door, he asks me again, "Do you believe I am telling the truth?"

"It doesn't matter as long as I get you the hell out of here." I open the door and leave.

⁘ ⁘ ⁘

Over the next few hours, Sanjay and I discuss my plan for a bail plea. I have given it a fair bit of thought in the little time I had, and I am hopeful it will work. Sanjay is impressed with my idea too but says there is a chance that the judge may still reject it.

"Did you have a chance to figure out if we have any friends on this case?"

"The DCP of Mumbai, Raghuram Dhawan, is a good friend of your father. I, too, know him from an earlier case."

"Can you find out if ankle trackers are available at the Trombay prison?"

"I think I can work out something."

"Additionally, we need to propose a very high bail deposit. What's the norm here?"

"The highest I have seen is five lakhs."

"Let's propose ten lakhs. Kishore has that kind of money. There is nothing that is more important right now."

"I will talk to him. But there is a risk that the prosecutor may propose the bail period be cancelled soon after the exams."

"Let's hope our case is done by then. Otherwise, we may have to look at a way of extending it."

"There is another problem. We won't have much time to gather counter evidence. Have you thought about how to proceed?"

Last night, I spent hours to come up with a strategy for our defence. This case is more complicated than I could imagine. And the evidence at best equanimous, if not outright against my client. But Sanjay's description of the prosecutor and her style of cross-examination has given me some ideas—we will give her a taste of her own medicine.

"For now, the only plan I have is to brutally discredit every evidence and witness that the prosecutor presents. We need information on every witness she may produce and every testimony that she will use. And then, we need to counter it or dilute it completely to tilt the odds in our favour."

Sanjay considers this for a few moments and then smiles. "Sounds like a plan. I will work on that. Let's meet Vishal tomorrow, at noon. We will have some time to plan out things until then. The prosecutor, Tara, will do something similar. She has a notorious reputation of ruthlessly assaulting the character of the accused."

I think about it for a few moments. The thing is, if Vishal is truly innocent, his conscience combined with the strength of my case should help us sail over whatever storm is coming at us. But if he is guilty, then justice should prevail, although I would still do my job to the best of my abilities.

"What we can best do is put up a strong front and throw in a fierce counter. I am not very well versed with the system here, but I know that if the arguments on either side are strong enough, it leaves enough room for the judge to consider an alternate point of view. We need to grab on to that small reasonable doubt, and then strengthen our case. Let's discuss with the Mehtas and Vishal, and prepare a set of people who can vouch for him."

At the end of the day, as I lie on my bed, I feel terribly exhausted and drained out. I gaze at the ceiling and think about Vishal's question. Do I believe he is innocent?

I am inclined to … because his story doesn't seem fabricated. He claims he used protection and seemed to have sincerely pursued the girl. So, what motive could he possibly have for murdering her? The other angle is that he appears to have been sexually frustrated after repeated attempts to get into her pants. He claimed that himself, that he wanted to take the next step and make it physical between them. Besides, we only have Vishal's side of the story. Perhaps he is a pervert and has violent tendencies. I consider talking to my father, but I know he may not be able to help. He hasn't been in touch with the Mehtas families for a while now.

I am normally good at getting a good measure of a person. I can easily call people on their bullshit. But now, I feel so out of my element. This new place, this new case, a new team, the new system—they are all messing with my sense of judgement. Added to that, my father makes me feel like a stranger in my own home. God, I miss my wife and kids. I need them all the more now. Tavi is coming back this Friday, the day of the hearing, and I hope that will boost my spirits enough to deal with the wreck that is going to follow.

The next day, Sanjay informs Kishore of our bail proposal, and he agrees to the amount without batting an eyelash. We also ask him to gather people, friends or relatives or workers—basically anyone who can vouch for Vishal's good character. Sanjay also manages to convince the DCP to make the ankle-tracking system available.

Thankfully, Kishore is able to pull some strings and ease up our visits to the prison, so we can walk to Vishal's room and get our job done. When we meet Vishal and explain to him what we have arranged so far, he looks hopeful. Sanjay has obtained the witness list, and Vishal gives me some pointers on each of them.

Toby Fernandez is the first guy along with a few bar waiters to have reached the crime scene. Vishal says he doesn't know the guy much. So, I will have to fight it out as and when it comes. Next is the girl's brother, Niraj, who filed the case against Vishal. Niraj is fiercely protective of his sister. He has a lot of respect within his community folks. He had discovered the couple before the breakup and had been totally against the relationship. He doesn't know that the couple patched up before the incident. He lives with his widowed mother who used to work at a garment factory to support the family, before her son graduated and found a job. I ask Sanjay to do a background check on this guy and gather as much information as possible. Mihir, the guy who was assigned with the task of making sure Nitya reached home, was last seen dancing in the bar crowd. He is a committed teetotaller who knew Nitya well, but Vishal doesn't know the guy much. We go over a few more potential witnesses, and then I question Vishal.

"You used protection. Did you guys plan it out?"

"My father taught me the consequences of unprotected sex are far too heavy. So, I am always prepared. But no. We didn't plan anything specifically. It was a spur of the moment decision."

"Did anyone else know you patched up?"

"No. My band knew we were being civil with each other. We kept it that way."

"Your mother mentioned you asked her permission to invite Nitya over?"

"Yes. But I never told her we got back. She may have guessed it though."

"This girl, Amrita, saw you leave with Nitya the day you both reconciled. Do you think she can testify for you?"

"She just saw me running after Nitya. But I never told her we got back. I was not sure if she could keep a secret. Besides she got busy with the film schedule after that. I am not sure if testifying for me will affect her career. You will have to just ask her. But she is quite unconventional and forthcoming, so she may just help us out."

I have a strange feeling about this girl. I make a note to explore the angle further and proceed with my questions. "So, what did you do with the condom?"

"Wrapped it in a tissue and flushed it in the bathroom."

I am not sure how I can prove this statement. It's one of the most controversial statements. The post-mortem reports prove penetrative intercourse and that protection may have been used. But the perpetrator's identity cannot be established. Sanjay and I have to explore all potential scenarios and be prepared.

Sanjay jumps in with his set of questions. "Were the two of you not scared of getting caught?"

"I was half drunk, and we were in the throes of passion. But I was aware enough to take her to the couch where we are least likely to be visible through the glass panel on the door."

"The girl was stabbed with a pair of scissors. It was the same pair that was on the office desk of the bar."

"I did not notice anything when we entered the room. Only that there was a dim light at the corner."

"There is evidence of the girl being manhandled. Around her jaw, on her throat."

"Oh God! I have no clue about that. All I did was mildly cover her mouth to muffle her screams, just to be safe."

"But … there was loud music playing downstairs, so there was no possibility of you guys being heard," I counter.

"I think … I think it was instinct."

"One last thing, the shirt you were wearing, it was drenched in blood, especially near the torso area. How so?" Sanjay chimes in. I swallow at the lack of empathy in his tone.

He stares at us in disbelief for a couple of minutes as if we have each grown two heads. He lets out a huff, shakes his head, turns to me and answers, "Mr. Bhargav, I stepped into the room to find my lover bleeding to death. Instinctively, I fell to my knees and clutched her body. That could have caused the stain."

We drill him a bit and leave for a visit to the crime scene. I take in the surroundings of the club and latch onto every detail I find suspicious. But nothing really appears to be insinuating an alternate possibility. DCP Raghu has accompanied us for this visit, and he keeps reminding me that there is nothing I could unearth here, because they have done a damn thorough job of collecting all evidence. I spend a little more time in the office room at the bar. The entire room has been left untouched and protected and will remain so till the case is closed.

I am sure this incident has affected the bar's business, but there is no alternative really. Poor guy, Toby Fernandez. I am told he recently spent quite a bit of money on revamping the exteriors with a paint job. I glance at the furniture in the room. Everything is where it should be. Not a thing out of place. I open the bathroom door and look inside. There is a sink, a commode, a bin and a ventilator window. Again, nothing out of place. We finish our business there and leave for the day.

The next day is spent on preparation and paperwork. Thankfully Amrita has agreed to speak in favour of Vishal.

On the D-Day, I wake up with a positive mind and prepare for the hearing.

CHAPTER 9

Ajay

The mood in the house is the exact opposite of the gloomy anxiety I am feeling on the inside. Tavi and the kids are on their way here from Singapore, and my mother is on cloud nine. There is a wide spread of breakfast dishes on the table. But I just have a sandwich and coffee. I am putting on my shoes when I hear some joyous squeals on the front porch. It suddenly occurs to me that my father is going to have a hell of a time till we move out into our apartment this Sunday. The thought of him frustrated with a noisy home brings a smile on my face. My daughter comes running to me just as I finish, makes herself comfortable on my lap and rests her head under my chin.

"Hi, Angel. I missed you. Are you tired?"

"A bit. I missed you so much, Daddy. Mommy missed you too."

I look up at my wife and she gives me a shy smile.

"How about your brother? Did he not miss me?"

And my older devil enters, looking at the hall and sniffing around. "What's for breakfast, Granny? I am so hungry!"

"But you will first freshen up," Tavi cuts in. "And no. Not allowed to grab a wafer on your way to the bathroom."

My mother laughs wholeheartedly, and my heart fills with warmth at the sight of my loved ones.

❖ ❖ ❖

After I say goodbye to my kids, I walk towards the parking lot, holding hands with Tavi.

"It's going to be okay."

"The public prosecutor is out for a kill. I am definitely nervous."

"If she is an elderly woman, make sure you be respectful to her no matter how sarcastic or condescending she is. The more you rile her up, the more she will be motivated to prove you wrong. So, do just the opposite."

I always ask my wife's advice while dealing with women, and she is usually right. I hope it's the same case now. I bid her goodbye and drive to the court. Nanda, the **PR** guy, has sent one of his team members to accompany me and prepare me a bit in case I must face the media. I tell him that I may not do well with on-camera performance, and he agrees to shield me from the media to the extent possible.

The Mumbai High Court is exactly as it was a decade ago, except now there are more garbage bins around the campus with a "Swachh Bharat" signboard glued to each one of them. I feel pity that the most important pillar of this country has been given the least attention. But some things never change.

Sanjay joins me, and together we make our way to the court hall. As we are about to enter, an older lady in a rich Kancheevaram saree walks towards us, her head held high. Without a doubt, I know it's the public prosecutor Tarakeshwari Rathod.

Her persona reflects her name.

See, I have a theory about names. Most often than not they give a message about the personality. When I was working in Singapore, we interacted with a prosecutor named Nancy over the phone. When I met her in person, she was exactly how I had envisioned, petite, sweet and reserved. Take my father, for example, Trivikram Bhargav. He sounds like a dominating man, tall and fierce, doesn't he? And that's exactly who he is.

My new adversary gives me a condescending stare as she approaches me. I remember my wife's advice and give her a humble nod in greeting. The judge arrives, and the session starts after the protocol announcements.

"Your Honour, we are here to represent a plea for the bail of Mr. Vishal Mehta, in the case of Vishal Mehta vs Niraj Harde."

"Mr. Bhargav, the plea was proposed during the last petition and rejected. Do you have anything new to say or any new developments that require to be examined?"

"Your Honour, we believe that there was insufficient representation during the last plea. We request your kind permission for another representation."

Tara interrupts immediately. "Objection, Your Honour. There are no new developments in the case. This is just a waste of the Hon'ble Court's time."

"Objection overruled. Mr. Bhargav, please note that this is your last opportunity for a bail plea."

"Thank you, Your Honour. Your Honour, the accused, Mr. Vishal Mehta, is a final year computer science engineering student, and his exams are scheduled in a few weeks. If he misses those exams, he loses an opportunity to graduate, have a career and become a resourceful citizen. The environment in the jail is not conducive for study and preparation, especially because the exams include practical assessments and the candidate will need his laptop and an internet connection to prepare. These things cannot be made available in prison. During the last plea, the main contention of the public prosecutor was that the accused comes from an influential family and can resort to underhanded tactics to affect the case in his favour. To prevent such a situation, we propose that the accused be mandated to wear an ankle tracker with GPS technology, which will allow the police to track his whereabouts at all times. This is in addition to the standard bail terms. In addition, the accused will be depositing an amount of ten lakh rupees as a security deposit, which may be forfeited in the event of the violation of any terms set forth in the bail."

"The proposal is reasonable, Mr. Bhargav. Ms. Rathod, any objections?"

"No, Your Honour." Tara grimly responds.

"Then, subject to the specified conditions, conciliatory bail is hereby granted to Mr. Mehta. Now, moving on to the next steps, the prosecutor and the defendant may present their respective arguments."

I enjoy a moment of victory at that announcement before the war begins.

Tara's first witness is Toby, the bar owner. As expected, he says that he saw Vishal holding the victim with a look of horror on his face. He only went in after he got the dreadful phone call over the intercom, and he has no idea what happened before. There was no one else in the room. Toby had not seen anyone else go into the room either. Tara states that the victim was with the accused at the time of the murder, so it directly implies he killed her. I raise my objection that Toby was ignorant of what happened before his arrival and so that cannot alone serve as a basis for charging the accused. My objection is sustained.

Next, she calls Vishal to the witness box. The thing is, I never prepped Vishal to alter his story before the hearing. I want to win without resorting to underhanded methods and so I had asked Vishal to answer everything just as he had narrated to me. Vishal takes the oath by the Holy Book, and the cross-examination starts. Tara asks him to narrate how the incident happened, and he tells her exactly what he told me. That tells me one thing—either he is really telling the truth, or he has fabricated a story and rehearsed it down pat.

"Mr. Mehta, for how long had you known Ms. Nitya Harde?"

"For about two years. We met during her first year at college."

"You were a couple for two years?"

"We broke up about this time last year and got back during December last year."

"So, you were together for a year before you broke up? Why didn't the two of you have any physical relationship during that time?"

"Nitya turned eighteen only a few weeks before we broke up, and we were taking it slow back then."

"And now you decided to speed things up?"

"We were just more comfortable this time."

"Why did you break up in the first place?"

"We were discovered by her brother, who was against our relationship. She did not want to go against his wishes."

"So, what made her change her mind and come back to you?"

"She told me she missed me and was now prepared to stand up for us."

"All this happened not too long before your graduation. Right?"

Vishal is confused and only gives a slight nod, but I know where

Tara is going with this.

"Did you have any other relationships, specifically physical relationships, during the period you were not a couple?"

"Yes. With a friend in London. But we were both drunk."

"Interesting. And you were drunk during this engagement with Ms. Harde?"

"I had a bit of alcohol. But I was definitely not drunk."

"Your Honour, it appears that Mr. Mehta was very keen to have a physical relationship with Ms. Harde, and since he was graduating, he decided to expedite things. We are not sure if the girl was willing, but it is clear that Mr. Mehta wanted to push his agenda, his desire further fuelled by his drunken state. And that's a crucial step towards a misdeed, Your Honour. That's all for now."

I have to nip this hypothesis in the bud before she develops it further. I walk up to Vishal with a counter in mind.

"Mr. Vishal, did you ever pressurize or force Ms. Harde to have a physical relationship with you?"

"Never. It was a big step. I waited for her to be sure."

"You had no romantic interests during the time of your breakup?"

"No. Just that one-night stand in London."

"Why?"

"Because I could never get over my feelings for Nitya. I loved her."

"Thank you, Mr. Mehta. Your Honour, the accused never forced the girl and waited for her to take the leap. He never pursued any other women other than Ms. Harde. That's hardly the psyche of a pervert."

"Your Honour. We are not implying that Mr. Mehta is a womanizer or a pervert. We are arguing that he was obsessed with Ms. Nitya specifically."

Before she can proceed, the judge adjourns the court for the day, and I am thankful for the break. It looks like Tara has quite a few tricks up her sleeve and lot of ammunition against Vishal. As I walk out, the Mehtas thank me for the successful bail petition, and I see hope flicker in Vishal's eyes.

CHAPTER 10

Ajay

Our next hearing is in the coming week. The weekend goes by smoothly, with our family spending some quality time together. We manage to move to our apartment successfully and the physical activity takes my mind off thoughts of young girls and their murders. I focus on my children and my wife. Most men in my profession usually look for a partner in the same profession. Perhaps because we believe we are a breed that requires special consideration and understanding. Surprisingly, doctors think so too. When I wanted to marry Tavishi, that was one of the key objections raised by my father. He argued that she wouldn't understand the pressures of this profession, and I would not have an emphatic ear, someone with whom I could share my day. He argued that Tavishi may similarly suffer from such a marriage. But that fear has been farthest from the truth. Because my wife is the smartest and kindest woman I have ever known, and we give each other valuable advice without knowing a damn thing about each other's professions.

From the first day we met, I have found her endlessly fascinating. There is between us an intensity and ease, a partnership and independence in everything we do. The complex things and the mundane tasks—be it decisions about our careers and investments in properties or preparing the morning coffee and tucking in cranky overtired children. Where I am practical and methodical, she is experimental and adventurous. Where I am subtle, she is disarmingly honest. She is the Ying to my Yang. I treasure the life we have built together, which is why I am so overcautious of any threats that may even slightly touch this sanctum. Which is also perhaps why this case is wreaking havoc on my peace of mind.

I don't usually discuss my cases with her owing to attorney-client confidentiality, but I do seek her advice on general aspects of my professional life. During the weekend, I give her a quick summary of the case and my predicament with my father. I also tell her about Vishal. The first thing she observes is that Vishal and I have a lot in common. Like our attitudes, love for music and like-minded fathers. While she cannot tell if he really did commit the murder, she agrees that pent up anger and frustration make people do insane things. And that is the root cause of my fear. I am scared that while it's possible for me to win the case, I might be preventing justice being served to an innocent girl. And in this profession, truth is a luxury we cannot afford. While there are laws like attorney-client privilege to protect the client, they often do end up being dishonest with their lawyers. Vishal may not be crookedly smart enough to play such games, but he comes from an influential and resourceful family, so I have to be cautious.

My earlier domain in cybercrime was a lot simpler. There were no lives involved. Only a lot of money and valuable information. I never spent too much time in the court, because most often than not, settlements were negotiated outside the court. And I have worked on both sides of the law, because sometimes, it's just about people who have made some bad decisions and are looking for a way out. I am bound by duty to believe the person I am defending, but the magnitude of what is at stake here weighs heavily on my conscience, and I fall into a restless sleep every night.

Sanjay has arranged for meetings with Vishal at the Mehta home for the next few days. Vishal's mother is adamant that her son stays at home, lest he should never return after the case. Sanjay is unable to join today, due to another case requiring his immediate attention. Frankly, I believe this case is my complete responsibility now. But I really do appreciate his help.

So today, as I am driving, I listen to *Bad Liar* by Imagine Dragons on the music system. I brood over how the lyrics aptly explain my predicament: *"I am a man of three fears—integrity, faith and crocodile tears."* I park my car and walk towards the house and hear faint music. I step into the office room to find Vishal lightly strumming the guitar, but he is deeply lost in unhappy thoughts. I almost see tears glistening in his eyes. When he hears my footsteps, he puts down the guitar in the corner and motions for me to take a seat.

"Is there anything I can offer you?"

"Some water."

He makes a quick call to bring some water.

"Music is a good distraction, you know."

"Except when it triggers some memories."

"Do you play well?"

"I have been playing for a long time. I am told I am not bad."

"What were you listening to now?"

"*Not A Day Goes By,* by Lone Star."

I change the topic and draw his attention to the matter at hand.

"Your father had arranged for a small press meet this evening. You, me and him. I am discussing the details with your PR representative.

You up for it?"

This PR shit is like a pungent icing on a burnt cake. Nanda has been badgering me for the statement he can release for the benefit of Kishore's fans and the public in general. I was cornered by the press during the last hearing, but thankfully, this guy intervened and got me safely to my car. He may have guessed my lack of experience. But this time I cannot escape, since everyone believes the next hearing will be a game-changer. I am not very good at making impromptu, uncontroversial, inconsequential statements to the public, unlike celebrity criminal lawyers.

Vishal responds with a small indifferent shrug.

Then we get to the main matters. "Vishal, Tara would most likely call Niraj in the next hearing. I want you to remember every little detail or conversation that you can recall. Please focus and remember."

"I told you everything. He caught us in an intimate situation once, and he definitely doesn't have a good opinion of me."

"How did he come to know about you? How did he know about your hideout?"

"I am not sure. I never asked Nitya about it."

"Why do you think he spoke to your father directly instead of approaching the principal?"

"I have a feeling Nitya had a role to play in that. She must have thought that it would adversely affect my studies if the principal took any punitive action. She must have begged her brother to reach out to my father instead. But I cannot be sure. I never asked her.

"Amrita has agreed to testify in your favour. Is there anything I should be wary of in regard to the nature of your relationship with her?"

"We are good friends. That's all."

"Do you think she had feelings for you?"

"It's possible. But she never pushed for anything. Why do you ask?"

"Because that may influence her statement in some way."

A strange look flickers over his face. I have a thought running at the back of my mind, but I park it there and focus on the remaining conversation. "Sameer has also agreed to testify in your favour. But there is a risk that Tara may strike down their testimonies since they come from people in your circle. We may have to bring in someone different from the group to affirm that you were always well-behaved with Nitya."

"Let me think about it. Lots of people knew about the relationship. But I am not sure they will come forward."

"All right. Give it some thought. I will call you tomorrow to discuss it further."

❖ ❖ ❖

Later that evening, we attend the press hearing. It is the three of us and a few reporters. Not that big a crowd. I have been thoroughly prepped for the tone and content of the statements, and I monotonously repeat what I have been told. Some of the reporters may have sensed my inexperience, which makes them ask me more questions. But Nanda is able to divert their attention and avoid some impromptu responses from me.

The next few days are spent preparing for the big hearing. Thankfully, Sanjay has unearthed some interesting facts about the victim's brother and that provides enough meat for us to discredit his statements.

As I go over the first information reports, post-mortem analysis and the rest of the evidence, a couple of things strike as out of place to me. First, there are no fingerprints on the weapon of murder, the scissors recovered from the victim's throat. Is it possible that Vishal really erased all evidence on the scissors? If he could plan these details so meticulously, he could have chosen a more suitable location to commit the crime and not the office room of a fully crowded bar. Second, a stabbing wound of such nature would have surely spilt blood over Vishal's shirt. I had called the investigating officer on this case, DCP Raghuram, to discuss this point. When the shirt Vishal was wearing was taken in for an examination, they found blood all over the torso. So, nothing conclusive could be drawn from that piece of evidence. Finally, the nature of the act itself that transpired between the two of them. The post-mortem report definitely confirmed some aggression in the way the victim's body was handled. There is evidence that her jaw and throat were squeezed tightly, and it's possible that the act itself was violent and rushed in nature, although no evidence is available to substantiate this.

The most disconcerting of this web of information and hypothesis is that Vishal's account of things seems to largely explain the evidence collected. He claimed he muffled her screams to avoid being discovered. He held the girl closely and hugged her body to his chest as soon as he stepped into the room to find her bleeding to death. He called on the intercom because his screams could not be heard over the loud music playing below. But the phone's receiver doesn't carry any fingerprints and that's a dead end there. But what confuses me is that he muffled the girl's screams, even though there was loud music playing down below. Toby confirmed that the music never stopped even for a few seconds during the party. Vishal claimed that his actions were instinctive.

Vishal's earlier question about my beliefs comes to my mind unbidden. I am lost in a tangled web of theories and counters, when I hear roaring laughter from my son, who is rolling around on the floor. He is watching some animation movie where a group of cartoon villains assemble and take a pledge together, "I am bad and that's good. I am not good and that's not bad." The scene playing in front of me brings an involuntary smile on my face.

I hear my phone buzz. It's Tavi.

"Hey!"

"Hey! I am at your mum's place. Aria is insisting on having dinner here. So, can you guys come over? Mum has prepared enough for all of us."

I pause for a moment. We have had dinners many times at my place, but tonight is going to be different. Because my father is around, and unlike all the other times, he cannot give random excuses to avoid us.

"Do you think it's a good idea?"

"Yes. Of course. There is enough food. Not to worry."

I get the message. My mother is somewhere close, and my wife doesn't want to offend her. Tavi got an opportunity to work as a visiting physician at a private hospital and my mother badgered her to drop Aria at their house when we are off for work. My mother is not losing a single opportunity to incentivize my kids to stay with them. Apparently, she got some new flower plants for their backyard and wants Aria to help her arrange them. My daughter loves flowers, diamonds and all things girly, so she had enthusiastically agreed.

Even before I can make up my mind, I hear my son wearing his crocs, all set to leave. The smartass got the gist of my conversation with Tavi, even though he could not hear her side of it.

⁜ ⁜ ⁜

Tavi looks nervous as she takes a seat at our dinner table. This is a new experience for her. Usually, our family dinners are boisterous with the kids narrating their day's tales and Tavishi and I diverting them with our questions and stories to make them finish the dinner quickly. It's the most enjoyable time of the day for me, second only to moments spent alone with my wife.

Today, she is not sure how to handle our kids. I am not nervous at all. If anything, I am looking forward to seeing my father being subjected to the fuss that's going to unravel in a short time.

My mother brings in a bowl filled with sautéed potatoes, which is the kids' all-time favourite. But before she can put the dish on the table, both the monsters start yelling: "Me first, Granny! No! Me first!" My mother looks worried. It is customary in my family to serve food to my father first. It's one of the many dinner rules. The other most important being little talking while eating. Only my father gets to talk, and he expects a firm "yes" in response, at all times.

"Let grandma serve your grandfather first and then it's all yours," Tavi says, wanting to avoid any confrontation.

"But what if he eats it all?" Aria asks worriedly. She can hardly eat two spoons but has her eyes on the entire bowl. I almost choke on my food. My father gives her a stern look with his brows furrowed and my mother starts serving the rest of us.

Aria is strangely calm now, watching my father intently. Suddenly, understanding dawns on me. She has never seen a man with a moustache, and I am sure she is wondering how my father is managing to eat without the food sticking to his moustache. I am about to interrupt when she gives a squeal, "Look! The curd is stuck on your moustache."

And there goes peace down the drain. My mother drops her spoon, and my son lets out a slow whistling noise. Tavi immediately reprimands Aria, "It's rude to stare when someone is eating. Please apologize to your grandfather right away."

"Sorry, I won't do it again."

For a fleeting moment, there is strained affection on my father's face. Aria is embarrassed by the whole episode, and she eats her dinner in silence. I want to cheer her up. She is just a little girl and my angel. She should always be smiling.

"Arka, what's the movie you were watching before we came here?"

"*Wreck-It Ralph*. 'I am bad and that's good. I am not good and that's not bad.'" He imitates the movie character in a deep baritone, and the kids burst out laughing.

I catch my father looking at them with—is it indulgence? But I know the man too well. He doesn't believe in proximity, banter and easy affection in relationships. I also notice his diet has reduced to a small proportion of what he used to eat earlier.

"Father, what's wrong? You are not eating enough."

"It's been like this for a few months. Nothing seems to be to my taste."

"You should try Mom's baked pasta with cheese. It's the best food in the whole world." God, there is nobody on this earth who can resist my daughter. I am sure my father will melt sooner than later. I notice that although he finished eating a while ago, he is still sitting at the table, watching all of us, especially the kids, with something akin to tenderness.

CHAPTER 11

Ajay

The next hearing on the case is scheduled for tomorrow, and Sanjay and I have gone through our arguments and cross-examination points in great detail. Preparation helps but not entirely, because our counters are based on the prosecutor's arguments. My strategy might just work—to discredit the witnesses, establish an absence of motive, and deem the available circumstantial evidence as inadequate. But it does have a crucial disadvantage. It exposes the case to a certain amount of subjectivity in judgement, which means success in this case will depend on whether the judge sees merit in my arguments. So, I have to tread very carefully.

My limited experience with this country's legal system acts as an additional barrier. I don't have enough credentials that could earn me some the goodwill with the judge. Neither do I know enough about him to guess what could possibly be his line of thinking. I have to solely rely on instincts. Then there is the whole mystery surrounding this case, which I am unable to untangle.

I decide to take a walk with my wife to take my mind off these issues. I am happy she has settled in well and am hopeful our family can grow closer to my parents in due course of time.

I am really blessed to have Tavishi as my wife. She is a great admirer of Sadhguru and often listens to his discourses. Right now, we are talking about father and son relationships in families. Apparently, my family is not unique. It's the same situation in Sanjay's house and even Vishal's house. The father and son don't get along too well. Tavishi tells me about Sadhguru's views on the father-son discord. The master says the problem is really two men sharing the same space and the same woman—a mother to one and wife to the other. And men are built differently, so they fight differently. Women have a different coping mechanism for altercations.

He may be right and my thoughts drift to my son and how we both would be with each other in the future. We are a great team together now, and I hope our relationship doesn't ever become strained. My wife thinks my father is changing too. She says the allure of grandchildren is too hard to resist, and my father will fall to their charms sooner than later. I really hope so, especially since this case is going to impact our relationship no matter how hard I try to win and no matter how hard he tries not to interfere.

The next day I head to the court, where Sanjay joins me. Today, we are expecting Tara to summon Niraj as a crucial witness to the case. His testimony is critical to this case because he was opposed to Vishal and Nitya's relationship and had caught the couple earlier in a compromising position. Tara will build her arguments around the fact that Vishal may have pursued the girl against her consent, and hence their altercation could have led to the murder.

The court session begins after the protocol formalities and Tara requests for permission to present the next witness. Niraj soon enters the witness box and Tara starts the examination.

"Mr. Harde, do you know Mr. Vishal Mehta?"

"Yes, ma'am. I caught him two years ago in the campus storeroom, *with my sister.*" No mistaking the icy bitterness in his voice.

"Can you please elaborate?"

"Mr. Mehta and my sister were in an intimate situation when I caught them."

"And then, what did you do?"

"I warned him not to contact my sister, and later, I spoke to his father to control his son and stop him from pursuing her again."

"Was your sister in touch with him after that?"

"No. My sister promised to break up with him. She took an oath on my father's grave to never connect with him again. And she never did."

"Objection, Your Honour. Mr. Harde cannot be sure if his sister really kept her word." Vishal told me nobody knew that they had rekindled their affair, but I have my own suspicions about the girl breaking such a solemn promise. But again, I suppress them. Duty. Honour.

"Objection overruled. Ms. Rathod, please continue."

"Mr. Harde, your sister was found with Mr. Mehta when the incident happened. Did you know they had got back together?"

"I am sure Nitya would have refused and resisted his advances. Mr. Mehta would have tricked her somehow."

"Why do you say so?"

And what comes out of his mouth yanks the ground from right under my feet.

"Mr. Mehta was obsessed with my sister."

"What do you mean, Mr. Harde?"

"When I discovered them last year, I overheard their conversation. Mr. Mehta was pushing my sister for a full-on physical relationship. But my sister did not want to."

What the hell is going on? I look at Vishal and find him nearly trembling, panic written all over his face. He never told me that Niraj overheard their conversation, much less those intimate details.

Niraj continues. "The couple was not aware I would be in town. I left my sister in the care of our family friends, but I was told she was coming home really late every day. If I were any late in finding out, I am sure Mr. Mehta would have taken advantage of my sister."

"Thank you, Mr. Harde. That's all for now, Your Honour."

And the ball comes to my court. I am still reeling from the shock of these revelations, and I have to take a deep breath to get myself in form. I approach Niraj, look him into the eye and start my examination. "Mr. Harde, are you married or in a romantic relationship with anyone?"

"No. I am not."

"Have you ever been in a romantic relationship before?"

"No." He is confused now and cannot tell where this is going.

"Objection, Your Honour. Mr. Harde's personal life is of no relevance."

"Your Honour. I am merely trying to prove a simple point. Mr. Harde doesn't have any experience with romantic relationships, so he is unfamiliar with romantic conversations and gestures that couples engage in. I am sure all of us who are in such a relationship would agree." There is a soft chuckle from the audience, and Niraj turns beet red at my statement. I also notice my father sitting in the last row. He is watching everything impassively. I don't know if he is evaluating me, but right now, I don't care.

"So, Mr. Harde overreacted after eavesdropping on such a conversation and conveniently assumed my client was obsessed with the victim. That's hardly a basis for judging Mr. Vishal's character."

"Objection, Your Honour."

"Overruled. Please continue."

I think the judge is intrigued by my line of logic.

"Mr. Harde, your mother was working for Jaipur Garments to support your family while you were still in college. Am I correct?"

"Yes."

"Four years ago, she met with a minor accident in the mill when her hand got stuck in the printing machine. Am I right?"

"Yes."

I am sure Tara is dying to raise an objection, but I know she is restraining herself lest she should earn the judge's reprimand. But I have got an interesting story here. Sanjay took the help of some of our paralegals and junior lawyers to do a background check on the victim's family, and when they found some leads, he used his connections to dig deeper. There was more to Niraj than he was letting on.

"Mr. Harde, the company paid your mother's expenses in full and even gave her one-month compensatory medical leave. Am I right?"

"Yes."

"But you challenged the compensation and instead filed a complaint with the Labour Commission. You asked for double the money as settlement, threatening to stage a protest if the demands were not met."

"Yes."

This guy looks nervous now. I am sure he suspects where this is going but cannot help it.

"The injury was not serious, Mr. Harde. It was a regular fracture and required a minor surgery. Your mother completely recovered in a month's time, just as the doctors had assured you. Yet, you exaggerated her condition to her employer. They were forced to agree to settle the claim as the company did not want any negative publicity just before their IPO."

"Yes, but the amount we asked for was nothing. We only asked for double the norm. My mother had been with them her entire life. Her loyalty and services are invaluable. They denied her an advance against her salary despite her repeated requests."

"Mr. Harde, the monies received were used to pay off your debt. Weren't they? We have bank records to prove that. It's not the magnitude, Mr. Harde, but the ethics of your actions that matter." After a brief pause for effect, I turn to the judge. "Your Honour, Mr. Harde here has a track record of using a situation to his advantage and his statements in the court may be taken with a very high degree of discretion. It's quite possible that he is waiting for the right opportunity to settle with the wealthy Mehtas."

"Objection, Your Honour. It's not fair to pass judgement against the character of the witness based his past actions." Tara's desperation is evident in her quick objection.

"Your Honour. The prosecutor has been doing just the same with my client all along."

"No, Your Honour. The situation here is different. Mr. Harde did not demand any money from Mr. Kishore Mehta when he called him to request his intervention in the matter of his son's affair."

"Your Honour, these moral-code violations manifest themselves only when there is need present. Besides, Mr. Harde could not have benefited from the situation when his sister was equally complicit in the affair."

"Objection overruled."

"Thank you, Your Honour. That's all."

Tara is not pleased with my line of arguments. Every character assault that she initiates will be met with an equal or more explosive response. That's our strategy. But I cannot be too happy about the outcome, because it's definitely stirring doubts about Vishal's innocence in my mind. Niraj's testimony came as a terrible shock to me. For one, Vishal never told me that the brother overheard their conversation. Maybe he thought that fact is not important. But I told him as clearly as I could that any detail will be critical to this case. And he omits this crucial one? Tara announces her next witness, Mr. Akshay Ahuja. He is not on the witness list that was shared with us earlier.

"Objection, Your Honour. This witness was not included in the witness list and cannot be called in as per law."

"Your Honour. We received his consent to provide testimony only yesterday, and his statements are crucial to the case. So, under Subsection 31 of the Law, I request that his testimony be admitted. Mr. Bhargav is fully authorized by the law to examine the witness in the next hearing if he deems it necessary, so no opportunity is lost."

The judge approves the witness, but I know this does not bode well. I look at Vishal who appears to have swallowed a lemon that's still stuck in this throat. What has he kept from me now?

Tara moves towards the witness box and starts with the questions as I hang on to every word coming out of their mouths to brace myself for any rude surprises.

"Mr. Ahuja, how do you know Mr. Harde?"

"We have been friends for many years now. We move in the same friends circles."

"In your experience, what kind of a person is Mr. Mehta?"

"Normally, fun-loving and carefree."

"What do you mean 'normally'?"

"Well, when he loses his temper, he is uncontrollable."

"Can you please elaborate?"

"During March last year, we were all at a party where my girlfriend teased Vishal about his ex-girlfriend, Nitya. They got into an argument and he used some very foul language with her. I intervened and asked him to control himself, but he argued that my girlfriend was the one that needed to be controlled and we got into a war of words. When I told him he was wasting himself over a worthless person, he punched me repeatedly and even strangled me. The force of his attack was so fierce I could not speak for a week and doctors told me I could have lost my voice if the choking had continued even a minute longer."

"Thank you, Mr. Ahuja. Does Mr. Mehta make a habit out of such violent behaviour?"

"Not until he met the girl. After he broke up with her, he was always short-tempered and angry. We also tried to avoid him as much as we could."

"Thank you, Mr. Ahuja. Your Honour, it's evident that Mr. Mehta has violent tendencies, especially when things don't go his way. You may please note that an angry and drunk Mr. Mehta choked Mr. Ahuja."

I am still reeling from the blow of this testimony. The judge asks if I have any questions, but I deny the opportunity because honestly, I know this guy is not lying. One look at Vishal is all it takes. Maybe he did not expect Akshay to come forward and entangle himself in this case. The judge adjourns the court for the day, and the hearing is postponed for three days.

CHAPTER 12

Ajay

Today, I have requested for the approval of the High Court to send the evidence, to the CBI Advanced Forensic Division for a relook at the scissors used for stabbing the victim. In addition to the witness testimonies and the available evidence, I need to discredit all the circumstantial evidence in the case, and I am hoping that the CBI report comes out in our favour. That could strengthen my case. That serves another important purpose. If the case receives CBI ratification, the chances of the judgement being challenged in the Supreme Court are dim. The report would be ready and available for the next hearing. Yesterday' proceedings totally threw me off my game. I am sure the verdict is now inclined as guilty and it would be a mountainous effort to tilt the scales in our favour. Meanwhile, Vishal and I have a lot to thrash out, and that's my first order of business.

We meet in the conference room of our office, both silently composing our thoughts. Sanjay is sitting on a chair facing the two of us, watching us carefully. Vishal eyes me warily and sighs audibly. I am sure he knows what I'm going to say, so he wisely doesn't speak first. I take a step back and perch myself against the table with my palms on the desk bracketing my hips.

"Do you know the punishment for abuse and murder in this country?" He doesn't respond, just swallows. So, I continue, "In your case, a lifetime. Which means that you will have to eat the stale bread you so relished the last time when you were in prison for the rest of your life. But I think you know that already. While I do appreciate your confidence in my criminal defence abilities, I am no magician. So, please spare me your feelings and explain to me what happened yesterday."

"Spare you my feelings? You have no fucking clue what I am going through right now. I have spared you enough of my feelings!" He yells, but I ignore the inappropriate language and jibe in his tone.

"The thing is, Vishal, if we don't get through this, you will have to go through much more on the stand. And there is no escape from that hell."

"I told you everything. Truthfully."

"You never told me about your little standoff with your friend from the same social circles."

"For God's sake, I didn't know he would come forward to testify and that incident will be connected to this case. I was drunk and don't even know what exactly happened that day. My father spoke to his dad, and I thought things were sorted out."

"Well, clearly not. For the non-controversial person you claim you are, you sure have made some enemies. You choked that guy because he said some bad things about your girlfriend? It could have been a criminal case. And why do you think he came out to testify now? What changed exactly? Some animosity between the families?"

"I spoke to father. Nothing happened. No contact. It's all business as usual. So, I don't know why he came forward out of nowhere."

"I think I know why, but you are not going to like it."

"What do you mean?"

"The guy genuinely believes you killed the girl, thanks to your earlier violent outburst with him. He wants to do right by the girl and also get back at you in the process. Two birds with one bullet."

"What?"

"Yes, you heard."

"But why would he get entangled in this mess? It would only paint a bad image of our social circle, as you put it."

Sanjay lets out a laugh.

"This whole social circle thing is as shallow and pretentious as it gets. Do you think people really care? Selfishness is a basic instinct. The guy is an aspiring actor, and his father is a second-rate actor at best. This is an excellent opportunity for him to boost his public image and at the same time malign your father's reputation."

"If he is so selfish, why didn't he just grab the chance when I attacked him?"

"Because that wouldn't get him positive coverage. Only sympathy at best."

"Then why didn't you apply your strategy on him yesterday? You didn't ask any questions. You simply let it pass."

"Because I didn't want to make a fool of myself and end up in the judge's bad books. Besides, what's there to argue? You choked that bloke in front of fifty people, and he let you go out of compassion."

He looks at me with a combination of fury and helplessness. I know he got the message loud and clear, and I need to move to the next order of business. I want him to confide in me, so, I go easy on him.

"Anyway, let's salvage this situation the best we can. It's our turn tomorrow and we have Amrita and Sameer. I am going to talk to her today to get the story straight. Anyone else I could call for a testimony?"

Vishal looks between Sanjay and me, and as if on cue, Sanjay walks out of the room and leaves us alone.

"There is actually something … and I am surprised Tara didn't bring this up yet."

"What is it?"

"I was caught drunk driving on one occasion and taken to the police station. A complaint was lodged, and we paid the fine."

"Okay," I say slowly. "That's not very significant. But did anything else happen?"

He bends his head to avoid eye contact and rubs his neck with his palm. There is a slight hesitation in his voice when he answers. "My father doesn't know about it."

"I understand, and I will see what I can do about it. So, what happened?"

"Another incident happened about two years ago, I was returning from a pub after celebrating my nineteenth birthday and I was driving the car. We hit a bike coming in the opposite direction. Fortunately, the man was wearing a helmet and did not suffer any major injuries. Just a hairline fracture and a few bruises. But the police were around, and they caught us. They issued a ticket and wanted to detain me at the police station. But I called my mother for help. She immediately came over, took the guy to the hospital and managed the situation with the police. Since he was also at fault, driving in the opposite direction, we could negotiate with him to not publicize the incident. My father was on a tour, and we never told him."

"Was there anyone else in the car with you?"

"Yes, Sameer was with me when this happened."

"Do you think the other driver will be forthcoming now … about what happened?"

"I am not sure about that, but I think my mother can help us."

Uh-uh. I look him in the eye and use my sternest voice to get the message across.

"Listen to me carefully, Vishal. You cannot interfere with any witness, direct, indirect, or anecdotal, with a ten-feet pole as long as this case is alive. Witness tampering is a serious offence. So please ask your mother to stay put and not act on it."

"Okay."

"Should I put that in triplicate for you?"

"No. I got it."

"Good. Now, about your friend Sameer. What's the deal with him?"

"I don't know. It's not as if he owes me or anything. But I have always been good to him."

"What do you think he can say that will help us?"

"We both used to play at the Oblivion Bar, and we would donate the proceeds to underprivileged children."

"That's very noble. I will make it a point to emphasize this."

"It's really not a big deal. I feel very uncomfortable with all this artificial gold-plating."

I let out a humourless laugh and brush it off. "And this girl … Amrita?"

"We were part of some beach cleaning drive. I am sure she did it for publicity. It received a lot of coverage."

"Okay. I will keep that in mind. Why did you not tell your father about the drunk-driving incident?"

"My father and I don't get along very well."

I suppress a dry chuckle.

"He doesn't like my carefree attitude towards life; he is a disciplinarian. When he found out about the first drunk-driving incident, he took my car keys and employed a driver to take me around. I was not allowed to drink for two months and not allowed to be at any party or even be at a friend's house after 11 p.m. It's not just these rules and regulations. He constantly nags me and never misses an opportunity to remind me how worthless I turned out to be."

I see more of myself in this guy each day. But the thing is, this age is a complicated period. While some guys can stew and brood and internalize their frustration at their fathers' overbearing ways, some turn extremely rebellious and instead, work on opportunities to get back at their fathers. Many parents in that generation don't know how to handle their sons. I hope our generation doesn't make the same mistakes and that I am a better father to my son.

My secretary calls me up to tell me that Kishore Mehta has come over to meet me and collect his son. Vishal's expression changes to that of frustration when he learns his father is joining us. I feel a little uncomfortable with the animosity between them, but I have no choice.

Kishore Mehta is definitely in a bad mood today. Maybe he lost a couple of movie offers because of this fiasco. He takes the chair next to his son and looks at the two of us. "So, what were you two discussing?"

I know he is itching to know his son's best-kept secrets. But the thing is, I have signed two different NDAs with the Mehtas. This was actually Sanjay's idea. He figured out there might be secrets that one of them might want to keep from the other, and since Vishal was not a minor, he was legally entitled to be a part of the contract.

"Just the usual, Mr. Mehta."

"Can I have a word with you in private?"

Vishal walks out of the room and Kishore Mehta begins. "Ajay, I was the one who proposed to put you guys on a fixed fee, not your father. He did not want a single cent from me. He felt he owed my parents, and hence me."

"Why are you telling me this, Sir?"

"My parents were in complete awe of your father. They wanted me to be like him. Successful, confident, formidable, powerful, everything. I hope I have been somewhat successful in meeting their expectations. And I too want the same for my son."

I am not sure where this is going and why I am being told about their family history. Maybe he just wants a sounding board. I have that effect on people. My wife says my face, voice and demeanour have a calming effect on people, and they feel like pouring out their troubles when they see me. If not a lawyer, I would have made an excellent shrink. When I travel, the passengers next to me become talkative and chew my ear off with their stories. My son's schoolteacher always makes it a point to meet me after everyone's done, so she can spend a few more minutes talking to me.

So now, I wear my shrink hat and listen to him.

"But you see, he is an only son and we had him after many years of our marriage. He and I are similar in many ways. But while my mother could control her protective instincts and ensured my upbringing was correct, my wife couldn't exercise the same control. My son can be very irascible and uncontrollable sometimes."

"Most fathers feel that way about their sons, Mr. Mehta. I know there is nothing unusual about your expectations for him."

He ignores me and continues. "I have had to deal with the consequences of his actions earlier as well. And I am not sure if many people would come forward and vouch for his good nature."

The message slowly starts to sink in. He is worried because he believes his son may have actually killed the girl. And he is not sure if we will ever win this case. I blink rapidly, not sure how to respond to him. "Sir, in my mind, your son is innocent. That is the truth I will give my best to prove."

He looks at me for a few moments, and I think I see a flash of hope passing over his face as he leaves the room.

❖ ❖ ❖

Kishore Mehta's visit has again messed with my sense of judgement. I feel like I am going in circles, with no end in sight. It's not that I am not used to dishonesty from clients. When I was in Singapore, I was once hired by a wealthy businessman to defend his underage son who was accused of hacking a dating company's website and stealing and misusing private information about their clients. We hired a top network security services company to analyse the traffic and could argue that it was actually a flaw in the dating company's app that led to the unintended breach of privacy. My client won the case with a hefty pay-out, because the company feared an adverse impact on its reputation should the case be taken to court and the breach be disclosed. We were all ecstatic.

But later, the boy confided in me. He had in fact very much hacked the App for fun but when it was discovered, couldn't come out clean because he was terrified that his controlling father would ground him or, even worse, humiliate him and cut off his mother's medical funds.

His confession did a number on me. Although I eventually reconciled with it because the poor chap was just a kid and because the other company was actually at fault, it taught me an important lesson. There is nothing called complete honesty in this profession. But here, it's not about money, it's about someone's life. If Vishal comes up to me Edward Norton-*Primal Fear*-style and says, "Hey dude! Thanks for saving my ass, but you see, I actually did kill the girl," I am surely going to lose my shit.

Sanjay and I discuss his meeting with Amrita, and he tells me Amrita's account of events is pretty straight forward. They met in London, are good friends, except for that one slip-up that night. They remained good friends even after Vishal returned to India. Amrita knew he would have patched things up with Nitya as she saw them together when she came to meet him, but she has not actually seen them together and Vishal never spoke to her after that, as she had to go back to Bangalore for an emergency. She has outrightly clarified that this is precisely what she will state in the court as well.

The thing is, while her relationship cannot be treated as romantic, there is a chance that all these testimonies may be dismissed as coming from the same social circle, and hence biased.

⁎⁎ ⁎⁎ ⁎⁎

I go home that day and find my wife watching an episode of *House*. It's our favourite show. I remember Dr. House, the protagonist in the show, teaching some life truths to his team. One classic quote from the series, that has lived with me *"It's a basic truth of the human condition that everybody lies. The only variable is about what."* This tenet resonates with my philosophy, and I am sceptical about most things coming out of people's mouths. As I take a seat on the sofa, my wife scoots closer.

"You did not have a great day, did you?"

"Yes. Sort of."

"Tomorrow is a big day."

"Yes."

"Something nice happened today. I met your father."

"Where?"

"Actually, he developed ear pain in the noon and your mother called me to check if I could drop by to take a look. So I went there on my way back from the clinic and took a look. It was a minor infection, and I gave him a few pills."

"And?"

"He tried to make a conversation with me as I was attending to him. He asked me about my work here, the kids' school, our home and other stuff."

"That's interesting."

"It's a small step, but I am happy we are connecting in some way."

"Thank you, Tavi."

"For what?"

"For trying when you don't need to."

"That's not true. This deserves my best just like everything else in my life."

"Thank you for thinking like that. I am not sure if I could be as accommodating if I were in your place."

"You would be. You are. You have been so accommodating and so forthcoming despite things here turning out to be so chaotic. You never lost your individuality."

"You would think that. You love me."

"I know that, and that's why I love you."

And that's when I know all is right in my world.

CHAPTER 13

Ajay

The next day morning, I take a shower and walk into my closet, hoping to see my wife and sneak in a few cosy moments. She is not there, and I am a little disappointed. But I quickly put on my clothes and walk towards the bed to find my daughter lying on her tummy on the bed, her legs in the air and her cute little chin resting on her palms at the foot of the bed. She gives me a mischievous smile.

"Mommy is saying bye to Arka."

"Good morning, sweetheart!"

"Are you not happy to see me?"

"I am always happy to see you. You are my sunshine."

She looks pleased, and before I know it, she is perched on my waist with her little arms wrapped around my broad shoulders. She cannot hold on for long, so I move her arms higher to rest around my neck. She gives me a sweet kiss on the cheek.

"I love your shirt, Daddy. Sky blue looks good on you."

"Thank you, sweetheart."

I carry her to the corner stand and put on my Rolex watch. The Rolex was a gift from my earlier firm upon my promotion to a partner. I was the youngest chap to have become a partner at Lawson's. The watch is one of my most treasured possessions. For one, it's exquisite. Made of platinum with a round black dial and a heavy oyster strap, it looks majestic and well-fitted on my bony wrist. And then, it represents my stupendous success in a highly demanding role. On the back cover of the watch, there is an inscription: "If you can dream it, you can do it." A famous quote by Walt Disney that the firm's founder swears by. Those words have always been a constant reminder of the power of human thought. Today, they present their message felicitously.

I put my daughter down to collect my wallet and turn to see my wife, dressed to freeze in a light pink saree. She looks delicious and divine, but she is up and ready early. I beckon her, and she comes right into my arms. I put my arms around her slim waist. I hear my daughter grunt at this display of affection between her parents, but she has seen a lot of this, and her reaction is just like this each time.

"What's up?"

"Well, I am coming to watch my husband in action at the court today!"

"Really! But how?"

"Yesterday, I requested your father if he could arrange it and he obliged."

My wife is a gem and I am sure my father would have realized she is special. He just needs to give her an inch, and she will take a mile of his respect. "That's nice, Tavi. My day already looks better."

We head to the court, and I am greeted by Tara in the hallway. She gives me a once over and remarks, "Good morning, Mr. Bhargav. Hope you are well prepared for today. I can see you are trying your best to fit into your father's shoes. That man is a legend, so you have a mountain to climb."

A commonly deployed trick to disarm people. Play the ambitious son against the successful father card. But she doesn't know me. I rarely get riled up. In fact, it's my composure that makes me formidable and frustrates people who try to make me lose my shit. I smile and give her exactly what she wants, "A man can hope, madam. I am only fortunate I got you as my adversary and nothing can be more propitious to my career."

She gives a small smile and a nod and walks away to the court hall.

✛ ✛ ✛

The judge enters, and we begin the session. It's my turn to present the witnesses, and I first call Sameer to the witness box. Sameer is a reasonably built young man with curious eyes. He is tapping his fingertips continuously, and occasionally his foot. Maybe he is nervous or because it's a common habit of musicians.

After he has taken his oath by the Holy Book, I approach him. "Mr. Sharma, how long have you known Mr. Mehta?"

"We are college mates. Same batch, but different streams. I am from mechanical engineering."

"How long have you known Ms. Harde?"

"Since she joined the college."

"Were you aware that Nitya and Vishal were dating each other?"

"Yes. All three of us were part of the college music band."

"Did you ever notice anything worrisome about their relationship? Specifically, Mr. Mehta's behaviour towards his girlfriend?"

"Never. They were a very loving couple. Mr. Mehta was always soft-spoken with her."

"How is Mr. Mehta in general? Has he ever been violent or rude to the people around him?"

"Not that I can tell. He is a compassionate man."

"Can you please elaborate?"

"Vishal and I play at the Oblivion Bar at Hotel Comfortel. All the proceeds are donated to a charity for children with autism. We both visit the institution and spend some time with the children there. Also, my younger brother, who is autistic, loves him and enjoys his company."

"Thank you, Mr. Mehta. Your Honour, as you may note, Mr. Harde has no history of abusive or violent tendencies. And his relationship with the victim had been cordial and normal. There is no basis to believe he had any malicious intentions as far as the victim is concerned. If anything, he is a socially responsible citizen. That's all, Your Honour."

It's Tara's turn for cross-examination. She brings the lapels of her coat closer. She is a woman on a mission, and I feel a bit jittery. "Mr. Sharma, did you know the couple broke up about a year ago?"

"Yes."

"Did you know they got back a few days before Ms. Harde's death?"

"No."

"How was Mr. Mehta during this period of breakup?"

"He was lonely and avoided us. He stopped playing for the band and did not join me at the Oblivion."

"So clearly, he was upset with the break-up."

"You could infer that."

"But you did not see much of him during this time?"

"Not until he came back from London. He was better when he returned and resumed his music with the band."

"How was he then?"

"Normal. He was polite and civil with Nitya during our music sessions."

This is going in the right direction, and I feel hope flickering in my heart, until Tara washes it away with her next question.

"Mr. Sharma, you were with Mr. Mehta in the car on 1st November, nearly three years ago?"

What's going on? How did she find out about this?

Sameer is nervous too as he responds hesitantly in a low voice. "Yes. I was in the car."

"He was very drunk, wasn't he?"

"Yes."

"That's very irresponsible behaviour. Do you agree?"

"Objection, Your Honour. That incident had no relevance to this case."

"It does, Your Honour. I am only countering Mr. Bhargav's point that Mr. Mehta is a responsible citizen. In fact, a ticket was issued, not once but twice, against Mr. Mehta for drunk driving."

"Objection overruled!"

"Thank you, Your Honour. Your Honour. I would like to emphasize that Mr. Sharma's testimony is not sufficient, because he is not adequately informed. For one, he never closely saw the accused during the period of their breakup, during which Mr. Mehta, in fact, assaulted another friend of his. We all heard Mr. Ahuja's account during the last hearing. Secondly, Your Honour, in Mr. Bhargav's own words, tendencies of moral misconduct need a trigger, and they don't manifest in public so easily. And lastly, there have been many instances of irresponsible behaviour of Mr. Mehta, under the influence of alcohol. The argument I am making is that Mr. Mehta had an obsession with the victim and under the influence of alcohol, was overcome with rage when his feelings were unrequited, and he murdered the girl. That's all for now, Your Honour."

Before I can respond, the judge calls for the next witness. Amrita is my last bet to salvage the situation, but I am not feeling too positive right now. As she makes her way to the witness box, I take a good look at her. Her brows are knit together in a frown, and she looks a little nervous as she studies the people sitting around. Finally, her eyes land on Vishal. She blinks a little and turns to me expectantly.

"Ms. Sunder, how long have you known Mr. Mehta?"

"Nearly a year. We met in London last summer."

"What's the nature of your relationship?"

"We are good friends."

"How would you describe Mr. Mehta?"

"He is friendly and easy-going."

"Did you know he had a girlfriend?"

"Hmm. Yes."

"Did you know they broke up?"

"Yes."

"Did you know they got back after a few months?"

"I guessed as much. When I came to meet Vishal once, I saw Nitya. Vishal ended our meeting shortly to go after her, possibly to speak and reconcile with her. I thought they would have patched things up, but I don't know for sure. I had an emergency to deal with in Bangalore, and never called him."

"During the time that you knew him, was Mr. Mehta ever furious or angry? Or did he ever misbehave?"

"No."

"Did he ever indicate any romantic interest in you?"

"No. He was never interested in me like that. He could never get over Nitya."

"That's all, Ms. Sunder. Your Honour, this is another testimony to affirm the accused was indeed committed in his relationship with the victim. It's highly unlikely that he would have committed such a heinous crime. That's all for now, Your Honour."

Tara has a smug look on her face as she starts the cross-examination, and I get an impending sense of doom. It's like a dull nagging sensation, and I can't place the exact reason. But I know things are going downhill.

"Ms. Sunder, your relationship with Mr. Mehta was only casual and friendly?"

Tara is either extremely perceptive, or she has perhaps done her homework well.

Amrita hesitates a bit before answering. "I ... we had a physical relationship one time, but it was not intended. We were both drunk."

"So, you both did not take it further?"

"No."

"Because neither of you was interested."

"Because Vishal was not interested."

"I see. So you proposed, and he denied?"

Smart woman. She knows she will hit a woman's soft spot when she brings up a rejection and make her defend herself and spill out more secrets.

"No. I did not propose. Vishal in his drunk state repeatedly called out the name Nitya, and I realized he still had feelings for her."

"Do you remember that night, Ms. Sunder?"

"Yes. Some parts."

"I am sorry to ask you some intimate questions, Ms. Sunder, but we need your help here. As you can see there is an innocent life that's been taken, and your statements are crucial to establishing the truth."

I want to correct her. It's "discovering" the truth but hold my tongue. Amrita gives a slight nod. I know there is no point in raising an objection. This is a crucial question, and my objection will be disregarded instantly.

"Was Mr. Harde violent with you?"

"Not violent … exactly."

"Can you please be more specific, Ms. Sunder? I am again requesting you to be as open as possible considering the value your testimony holds."

"I … I am sorry I can't explain it correctly. I can just say Vishal was agonized and was venting out his frustration over the loss of his love."

"Thank you, Ms. Sunder. Your Honour, this clearly affirms that Mr. Mehta, in fact, has a tendency of violent expression, especially under the influence of alcohol. This character trait serves as a strong motive for the crime committed by Vishal."

"Objection, Your Honour. Ms. Rathod is extrapolating and twisting the witness' statements to align with her arguments."

"Objection overruled. Mr. Bhargav, let's not undermine the facts here. Before we proceed with the arguments, let us examine the report received from the CBI Advanced forensic research division. The findings may be read out."

The clerk brings over the report and the summary of findings are read out for everyone's benefit. "After a thorough analysis of the instruments submitted for evaluation, using radiation screening methods, it is hereby stated that the findings are equivocal. Presence of fingerprints cannot be conclusively established, and it is recommended that the findings be corroborated and triangulated with other evidence found at the site of the incident. This report alone, in its full capacity, cannot substantiate the use of the weapon for the crime in question."

The dull sensation of doom is intensifying. The report basically means that either nobody used the scissors, or someone washed the scissors after use, or whoever used it wore gloves. But the latter is not possible since no gloves were found at the site of the murder, and Vishal never wore gloves to the club. After the report is read, Tara stands up to deliver her arguments.

"Your Honour, I would request your permission to borrow the judgement and findings from the Wadhwa–Rufus case last year. It may be kindly noted that the weapon of murder that was used did not carry the fingerprints of the accused because his hands were sweaty. Since direct witnesses to the crime came forward later to testify against the accused, the analysis report of the CBI was not needed. Nevertheless, the CBI report highlighted the probability that fingerprints may not have formed because of perspiration. It may be noted that the couple were dancing for a long time, and then the two were engaged in a passionate encounter. It's quite possible that the palms of the accused were sweaty. In fact, the police officer, in his account of events, had mentioned that the accused was terribly scared and profusely sweating when he was first found in the office room. Another important aspect to note Your Honour is that the telephone receiver did not bear any clear fingerprints either and the forensic lab inferred that this is quite possible because of perspiration"

"Your Honour, whatever is being said is an application of an observation pertaining to a different case and cannot be immediately applied to the current case. I humbly submit that the operative word is 'probability', and it is not quantified. I request the Hon'ble Court to not solely rely on such a probabilistic event."

"Your Honour, in his efforts to exonerate the accused, the defence seems to be ignoring an important factor. We all agree it is not a suicide, so someone obviously committed the crime. Who could possibly murder a simple uncontroversial college girl who has no known enemies?"

The judge looks at both of us, sighs and asks us to take a few moments to summarize our arguments and findings. Tara and I take our seats, and there is absolute silence in the hall for a few moments.

Tara goes first to deliver her concluding statements. As expected, she is composed, confident and thorough when she summarizes her arguments. She must have done this a hundred times now.

"Your Honour. An innocent girl was brutally murdered on a night when she was partying with her friends. A girl who was loved by all, had a good academic record, was talented in many ways and would have made her motherland proud of her achievements and contribution if only she had lived longer. This city and this country are mourning her loss and are desperate for justice. This girl was found dead with scissors stabbed into her throat, her body disrespected, and possibly violated and abused. The scissors don't have any fingerprints on them. The only person present at the crime scene was her previous lover, the accused. Surprisingly, her lover claims they had a consensual sexual encounter right before the incident. He found her dead when he stepped into the room after using the bathroom. The accused is known to be a generally good man however, there are certainly a few incidents of angry outbursts and physical assault. I would also like to emphasize that he hails from an influential and resourceful family. He had a privileged and informed upbringing, and hence, the ways and means to be thorough at the crime. Everyone agrees he was frustrated over the victim's rejection and severance of their relationship. I would like to once again borrow the famous Wadhwa case, where the weapon of murder doesn't carry any evidence, and the suspect was acquitted of all charges. It is only when the witness came forward after many months that the case proceeded, and the suspect was found guilty of the crime. Unfortunately, the girl died in the meantime, and her mother committed suicide.

"In this case too, we have a similar situation. Unfortunately, there cannot be any more witnesses to help us reach a definitive conclusion. But Your Honour, there is a crime, there is a victim, there is a suspect and there is a motive for the crime. If the Hon'ble Court acquits the accused, not only are we denying justice to the victim but also releasing a dangerous criminal into the society. Hence, Your Honour, I request the Hon'ble High Court to take into account these considerations and pronounce the accused as guilty and provide the victim and her family with justice and closure. I rest my case. Thank you, Your Honour."

The judge jots down something and requests for my summary. I compose myself and gather my thoughts as I rise from my seat to deliver my statements. When the judge gave us a few minutes to conclude our arguments, I realized something. This is perhaps the first time in my life that my words hold paramount value. Because they have the power to influence the verdict and save a life. There is a power about that realization, because all my thoughts declutter. I feel strangely enervated and a sense of calm and clarity emerges, along with a feeling of humility. I begin:

"Your Honour. Whatever the public prosecutor has said is an apt description of the current situation, and I wouldn't have summarized it differently. But, Your Honour, whatever has been said may not be the truth. Because the truth is absolute. As a great man once said, the truth is not for comfort; it's for liberation. And it is out there, eternal and untainted. On the other hand, justice, Your Honour, needs a proof of truth. And here, Mrs. Rathod and I are trying our best and expending our efforts to formulate or unearth that proof. But, Your Honour, unlike the truth that is sacrosanct, our proofs are not. True, they are built from logic and reason, but they are also tainted by our perception and experience.

"If every wealthy, influential and resourceful man in this country had a penchant for malice, this country would forever be poor and miserable. And my defendant here is a son of this country too, with a good academic record, multifaceted and talented, someone with the potential to make this country proud with his contributions. True, he had a privileged upbringing and is more informed, but there is no evidence that he is any more informed in the ways and means of committing a crime than any average person.

"But it is natural for us to immediately apply our experience and knowledge to solve a problem. It is natural for us to stereotype, because that makes it easy for us to understand people and assign a motive to their actions. And that is how our proof of the truth comes to be. Such a proof will not succeed in discovering the truth. It will not achieve liberation. It will at best give us the small comfort that we did our best.

"Your Honour let's not contend ourselves with that comfort. Because that is not complete justice to a daughter of this country, who deserves liberation. That's all from my end, Your Honour."

I look into the eyes of the judge, humbly nod, and take my seat. The judge looks at me for a few moments with a semblance of respect and admiration. Then, he closes his eyes for a few moments, let's out a deep breath and makes the announcement

"After taking into account the arguments and testimonies provided by both the parties, I hereby grant an additional time of one week for pronouncing the verdict. The Hon'ble Court believes that there is merit in Mr. Bhargav's plea, and accordingly, finds that the case requires more time and consideration. The parties are requested to collect and analyse the case facts further and present additional arguments if any during the next hearing, which shall be final as far as the case is concerned. The court is adjourned."

I let out the long breath I have been holding. This is a small victory, although I am not sure what to do with the additional time. But I have surely made a positive impression on the judge, and I am glad that my first case in my country has earned me some respect. I look at my wife and father, who are waiting with the rest of the audience. My father gets up to leave as Tavi comes to me with an understanding smile.

We leave the court hall hand in hand.

CHAPTER 14

Vishal

Everyone in the courtroom starts vacating the Hall and my father's security guys keep themselves close to us as we are escorted outside to the parking. Nanda makes his way to me and whispers, "The media is thronging outside. They will ask you a lot of questions, but you don't have to answer anything. We already prepped your dad. He will answer on your behalf. Remember, Vishal, don't say anything. Just stay put."

"All right."

I am totally exhausted, and I don't think even an earthquake can shake me from this lifelessness I feel. So, they don't have to worry about my loose tongue.

As we approach the exit hallway, a few reporters eagerly approach us to get some sliver of information to feed their channels.

"What are your thoughts, Mr. Mehta?"

"What are you planning to do now that the case is postponed?"

"They say that you may have played a role in today's decision to delay the case. Is that true?"

"Why did you hire an amateur like Ajay Bhargav for this case? Is it because other lawyers refused?"

"Are you hoping for a settlement, Mr. Mehta?"

My father, walking in quick paces, comes to a halt and finally answers. "There is no question of any settlement. My son is innocent, and he will be acquitted shortly. Now, please excuse us."

"Why is Vishal Mehta not answering any questions? He is an adult! How long are you going to hide him like this?"

I look up at this blunt reporter. She is from JantaTV, I think. She looks feisty and determined to get some answers.

My father stops again and answers. "Can you please be more considerate? My son is obviously going through severe trauma, and he is unwell and exhausted. We don't want to stress him anymore."

She scoffs at my father. "Considerate? Your son stabbed an innocent girl. What does he need to recover from? The monstrosity of the crime?"

Those words wake me up with a jolt. Nanda immediately corrects her. "Madam, don't cross the line and be presumptuous. Nothing has been proven yet."

And then all the reporters, fuelled by this woman's remarks and our attempts to rebuff her, crowd around us and storm us with questions. "Because you are not allowing it to be proven. Vishal Mehta, why are you not answering? Is your father worried you may say the wrong things and dig yourself deeper? Tell us about your plans. The odds are obviously against you. Are you going to approach Mr. Harde for a settlement? The girl is no more, so it doesn't matter how much you both negotiate."

The last sentence comes out of the same reporter's mouth. A wave of fury washes over me, and before I can stop myself, I pounce on the mike and camera in front of me and throw it away. Immediately, my father's security guys grab me by my arms and pull me away from the reporter. I kick and scream and yell at her. "Of course, the girl is dead! Do you have no compassion at all? Someone should teach you kindness, you heartless bitch!"

But my screams and profanities are muffled by a strong hand around my mouth and no word comes out clearly. The reporter has a look of terror on her face, as I am grabbed away from the media and towards the parking lot and pushed into my car.

⊹ ⊹ ⊹

Back home, I collapse on the sofa of my drawing room. Oh God! Why are people so insensible? Why have I become the object of everyone's scorn and disgust? Why is fate playing these sick games on me?

I eye the shelf in front of me and open the door to grab a bottle of whiskey. As I take a big swig, a hand snatches the bottle and hurls it on the opposite wall. The bottle shatters into a hundred pieces with a loud bang.

"You are not taking a single sip of alcohol again."

"Dad!"

"Shut up! Why did you not tell me about the accident? And have you lost your mind? You nearly assaulted the reporter."

"She deserved it! That fucking bitch!"

I hear the sound of something snapping and feel a powerful impact on my face. My cheek throbs from the sting of the slap I just received from my father. This is the first time he has hit me.

"What …"

"Not a word. Because if you speak, there is a chance we will both end up in prison. You are a complete and utter disappointment. You know what? If you had any shame you would have just admitted to the crime and served your sentence in prison instead of putting me through this nightmare. Do you have any idea how much I am fighting to get you out of this mess you have made? How much money I am spending on lawyers, on PR and everything else? And you do some stupid reckless shit like this and it's all gone … Boom! Ajay fought tooth and nail today to buy us more time and paint a good picture of your character. You do something like this, and all his hard work is ruined! And now you want to drink? And then do what? Drive your car and smash it somewhere? Or find another girl and treat yourself to some sick pleasure?"

The rage consumes me again, but I am physically incapable of acting on it. I feel weakness take over and my father leaves my pathetic self alone.

When I was younger, my mother once took me to play on a beach in Australia. I hadn't learnt swimming then and when she was applying sunscreen on my back, I mischievously just ran into the sea to play with the water. As the waves crashed against me, I lost footing and a huge wave pulled me inside. I felt myself drowning as I desperately tried to hang on to something to keep me afloat. That was the moment I knew what fear and helplessness were. The wave was so powerful, ruthless and unforgiving against my small and frail body that I couldn't come up for air and call for help. And I surrendered. I let it take me wherever it wanted and closed my eyes in defeat.

I woke up a few hours later in a hospital bed. Apparently, I was saved by a kind surfer who immediately resuscitated me, helping me empty my lungs of water. He then called for emergency services. I don't remember how and when I was rescued. But I remember the feeling of drowning very well. So well that even after all these years, that was my worst nightmare. That is, until I laid eyes on Nitya's dead body.

Today is the closest I have ever been to that feeling of powerlessness. I just want to give up and let providence take me away, wherever I am headed. I cannot fight any more. Because there is nothing I can hang on to. No one I can hold on to, who would be there for me, who would stand by me. Sure, my mother is on my side, but her support is out of maternal love, not out of any real faith in me.

How have things gone so horribly wrong? How have I destroyed myself like this? When did I become such a liability to myself and others? Maybe my father is right. I should be in prison. Ajay fought for me. If he had won, I would have been acquitted and the case would have been closed for good for lack of sufficient evidence. What does that achieve? Who does it help? Maybe I should have admitted to the crime. I fully deserve the punishment. Oh God! Why am I wasting everyone's life?

And my father has deprived me of the only thing that could have helped a tiny bit. I look at the shattered pieces of the bottle in front of me and laugh.

Because right now, they look more intact than my brutally broken heart.

Ajay

The success today, albeit small, feels oddly unfulfilling and has left me exhausted and worn out. It feels like I have climbed the mountain with great effort only to reach the top and not know where to go from there. I just want to listen to some soulful music and forget about tomorrow. But I know that cannot happen because, well, for one, I still have a case to fight and have no damn clue what to do next. My secretary, Roopa, brings a cup of steaming coffee and places it on my desk with an understanding smile.

"Anything else, Mr. Bhargav?"

"No. I need some time for myself. Please do not allow any visitors."

"Sure, Sir."

I let out a deep breath, recline my chair, crane my head backwards on the headrest and turn on the remote of my music system. The soothing sound of Yanni's violin slowly relaxes my nerves and I close my eyes in nirvana.

I think it's been just about ten min into my blissful oblivion, when I hear Roopa's voice. I open my eyes to find her scurrying into my office with a worried look on her face.

"Mr. Bhargav, it's Kishore Mehta. He says he wants to speak to you urgently."

Oh God! What now?

"All right. Put him through."

"Hello, Mr. Mehta. What is the matter?"

"Ajay, there has been a bit of an emergency, and I need your help."

"What is it, Sir?"

"There was some altercation between the media and Vishal and things are not looking good at the moment. We need you to give a statement to assuage them."

"Mr. Mehta, I am sorry, but I am not very good at this. I have never done this before. And the media here are like helmet sharks. I can't handle them. Definitely not right now."

"Please Ajay, you need to do this. Nanda will guide you. Don't worry, it's not as bad as you think."

"Mr. Mehta, I …"

"Ajay, Vishal scared away a female reporter today when she provoked him, and things are not looking good. If we don't give them something, they are going to blow this up and damage our chances of winning."

"Mr. Mehta, on one condition. You must join me. I cannot do this all alone."

"All right. I will be there. But you must do a lot of the talking. I am not in their good books, and they are eager to listen to something more definite and suggestive. You are our best bet."

"When is the press-meet?"

"Today evening."

"Okay."

I rest my head on the desk and take a few breaths. What have I gotten myself into? And what's wrong with Vishal? Why does he have to behave like an errant child? Immediately, I am overcome with regret over my decision to come to India. I cannot help but be angry with my father for making me go through this. But again, I resign to my helplessness.

⁂

A while later, Nanda comes hurriedly into my room, sweating and restless. He doesn't even greet me when he enters—just walks over and puts some papers on my desk.

He takes me through the process. "These are statements you can say, and these are statements you cannot say. The idea is to give them information but not reveal too much. It's good to keep them guessing and be non-committal, always. And always speak highly of the Mehtas."

He goes on for a while and pauses, waiting for me to say that I understand. I am too worked up to speak, so I just give him a nod. We head to Kishore Mehta's office to join him for the press meet. Mehta has quickly organized a dinner and some booze for the press in an effort to do some damage control. Nanda has insisted that I stay back for dinner and discuss life in general but don't reveal any personal details. He has given me a list of topics I can scope and talk about. Despite his best efforts to prepare me, I don't feel prepared enough, but there is only so much all of us can do.

The press assembles, and I am taken aback when I see at least twenty of them. This is much larger than the gathering I had to face the last time, and now I have to respond to their questions directly. I don't remember ever talking to a single reporter or journalist in my life.

We all take our seats and Kishore Mehta thanks them for their support, professionalism and cooperation. Internally, I laugh, because that's exactly what is missing here. The initial questions are directed to Kishore Mehta, and he answers them until, after a few minutes, he purposefully directs one question to me.

I brood over the question a bit before responding. "Ah. Yes. We are going to review the evidence provided to us to see if there are any missing pieces. That is definitely one of our starting points."

"Mr. Bhargav, this is your first criminal case in India. Are you confident you will succeed in winning this case?"

That hurts, but I answer anyway. "I am thankful to Kishore Mehta here, for giving me this opportunity. TS partners has very strong credentials in the criminal law space and our team is fully on board with this case. I have had a very successful career as a cybercrime lawyer myself, and I know how things work. We are fully prepared and confident of winning this case."

"Your father was a prior member of the Special Advocate Bench. Do you think you will take his help in replacing the judge on this case?"

"No. We are not doing anything like that."

"Mr. Bhargav, you are a father too. How does it feel defend the accused of a murdered innocent young girl?"

I cringe at the mention of my parental status, and I am flustered and confused for a few moments. This is much harder than I thought. "I will defend my client to the best of my abilities."

"What about justice, Mr. Bhargav? Are you not concerned about that?"

"I ... I am fighting for justice. To my client here, who is wrongly accused of a crime he did not commit and ..."

"The scales are tilted, Mr. Bhargav. The famous Kishore Mehta against an average Indian family. You are surely at an advantage ..."

And I cannot focus on anything she says after that. I feel claustrophobic and smothered and am running out of politically correct, unrevealing diplomatic answers.

I think Nanda notices my discomfort and predicament, because he finally intervenes. "Ladies and gentlemen, Mr. Bhargav has a lot of work to do, and we will be thankful to conclude this meeting now. We will be releasing an official statement tomorrow with more information on our plans. Please join us for dinner and drinks. And thank you again for your understanding and cooperation."

The next hour is spent on socializing and walking around. I take a few sips and nibble on a few snacks, but my capacity to continue with this charade is quickly running out. I realize I need to get out before I blow this out of proportion. I feign a stomach-ache and excuse myself from the rest of the dinner. I cannot wait to confront my father about this situation that he has so conveniently created for me and sort out things with him. But I don't find him at home; he is visiting his friend who lives across the city.

I am frustrated and I need to extract myself from this battle I am fighting within, but I really don't know how. My father has gone ahead and complicated my uncontroversial life with this damn case, which I cannot seem to unravel. I am fighting too many challenges— my discomfort with criminal cases, dilemma about Vishal's innocence, inexperience with the legal system here, new people, my sour relationship with my father, and to top it all this media frenzy that is only adding fuel to the fire. I want to quit so badly and ask my father to hand over this case to someone else. But I can't because I know how important this is to him. I can't because I never back out from a challenge, especially when it involves my work. I am not too proud to lose battles for my family or admit defeat in arguments with my wife. But my career is something I never turn my back on.

My mother comes to me with a worried look on her face.

"What happened Ajay? Are you all right?"

And she has just opened the floodgates. I pour out my worries to her. "No Mom, this case is taking a toll on my sanity and peace of mind. Father just handed this over to me because he owes it to the Mehtas. It's an abuse and murder case involving the Mehta's son. He is wealthy and influential and reckless and irascible. I don't even know if he is innocent, and I am defending him. He is accused of murdering a young girl, and I have a daughter. Imagine the havoc it is wrecking on my conscience. And today, I had to face the media. They think I am a money-mongering corporate lawyer out to negotiate a settlement and drop the case against my defendant. I am just back from Singapore and father has dumped this mountain of a responsibility on me. I cannot back away from this. Father promised he wouldn't interfere, and I appreciate the sentiment but that's not a great help. I want to ask him why. I came here to get some much-needed answers, and he isn't there. He is never there when I need him."

"The Mehtas raised him, Ajay, and he always considered Kishore as his younger brother. The thing is, Kishore never reciprocated your father's efforts to forge a relationship. Or maybe your father didn't know how to forge a relationship ... but they grew apart after their parents' demise. And after all these years, when Kishore called him up for help, your father believed this is the one chance to make things right between them. But I understand where you are coming from. Your father has always been harsh on you. Believe me, he has missed you so often during the last few years ... he just didn't know how to reach you. And now this case happened—"

Something strikes me, and I cut her off. "Mom, is that why you asked me to come? Is this case the real reason I am here? Tell me the truth mother, or so God help me, this has gone way past the redeemable stage."

"Ajay! No! I would never do that to you. Neither would your father. He is not your enemy, for heaven's sake. Don't let these negative thoughts rule your mind, Ajay. Let me talk to your father. It's high time he takes care of his family."

"No, mother, that's okay. Don't stress yourself. What use is it anyway?"

"I know your father, and I know you too. Let me take care of this."

"Whatever, Mom. I am not too hopeful. I am going home now. I am just tired."

"Take care, Son."

"You too, Mom."

CHAPTER 15

Ajay

I return home to find it empty. My wife and kids are at the community clubhouse, and she has dropped a text to me asking me to attend to some electrical issue in the bathroom. I almost tell her I am drained out and need to rest but realize that this mundane task will help me take my mind off the life-altering arguments presently occupying my head. Stress has different effects on different people. Some people yell, some withdraw. But I become unbearably cynical. I may also be going a little crazy. Because despite the hundred different distractions I could engage in, I decide watching an electrician fix my bathroom is going to be effective. Unfortunately, I am so wrong, and this case appears to be haunting me everywhere. Because the electrician working in front of me right now throws furtive glances my way every now and then. He probably knows who I am and is now being judgemental about my decision to defend a wayward rich bastard who most likely murdered an innocent girl. This is the media's unsolicited blessing to yours truly.

The thing is while we have mostly settled in our new home, there are still some punch list plumbing and electrical works that need to be done. The exhaust fan in the guest bathroom is not functioning, and he is examining it as I wait on the other end near the washbasin. I don't know if it's my recent adventures with the media or my personality in general, but this guy is very talkative as he explains what he is doing at every step.

"Sir, some wiring issue. I am going to replace it but it's better to bring the connection from outside, to avoid any moisture touching the wiring."

"Okay. Do whatever is needed please."

He opens a few latches and the entire vent adjacent to the exhaust comes apart in a matter of few moments. I am a little surprised.

"Hey, it's so easy to open."

"Yes, Sir. But don't worry the latch is on the inside, so no security issues there. Some bathrooms come without any latch at all. Those are the ones that are dangerous."

A strange thought crosses my mind at this, but it quickly vanishes when he interrupts.

"You must be stressed out from the case, no? You just moved here, and the media is all over you."

"It happens sometimes. But thanks for the concern."

"Did you meet Kishore Mehta, Sir?"

"Many times, and yes he is handsome, but a normal guy like most of us."

"I am a great fan of the actor."

Before the conversation delves further into acting skills and then Bollywood gossip, I excuse myself and go to the drawing room. The electrician is done with the work in a few minutes and leaves. I am now alone and sitting in the drawing room of our house with my thoughts scrambled and unclear. There is a commotion at our door, and I turn to look at Tavi and Vishal step in together.

"I met Vishal in the lobby. He wants to have a word with you. I will take the kids out for some time."

I look at Vishal and motion him to follow me to the office room on the first floor of the house. The room is my place for contemplation and solace. There is a music system, some souvenirs from the football tournaments I had attended, a shelf with top-quality wine and a refrigerator that stocks whiskey, beer, and scotch. I don't drink often, just a few sips of wine now and then, and scotch on the rare events when I require something stronger.

I turn to Vishal to see him eyeing the refrigerator and the minibar and ask him, "Can I offer you something to drink?"

"Something strong, if you don't mind?"

I get us two glasses and pour a generous amount in one and a little in another, and hand over the fuller one to him. He takes a sip, and I take the opportunity to observe him. He doesn't look good. His eyes are puffy and red, and there are dark circles below them, maybe from lack of sleep. He looks pale and dehydrated but determined.

"What have you thought about the case?"

"I am still thinking."

"Working out more ways of elevating my moral code?"

"Vishal, what's going on?"

"The judge gave you more time to figure it out after your impassioned speech about truths and proofs. So you are rejoicing in your victory, huh?"

"You seem to be quite thankful for someone who just got pushed a little farther from the gallows."

"Oh yeah. A few days of paradise to check off items from my bucket list. Can't tell you how happy that makes me."

"Care to tell me why we are sharing these pleasantries? As you so rightly reminded me, I have a case to fight. Still."

"You don't get it, do you?"

"No, I don't."

"All of you are selfish players just pushing their agendas, while my life is being pawned out. You, that woman Tara, my father, each and every one of you. Your only concern is winning the case, and whether I am guilty or innocent, it doesn't matter. Tara builds up a theory to prove me guilty, and you formulate another to paint me innocent. There is a war of words, my past is ruthlessly dissected, and every action is studied and retrofitted to suit one agenda or the other. Everything I have done has a motive and strangely very relevant to the case."

"I am sorry to tell you this, but you have been accused of *killing* someone. I hope you realize the magnitude of that offence. And we may be callously dealing with your past transgressions, but that's the only way out."

"Is it? The only way out? And what does it achieve? Either I am in or I am out. If I am out, then there is really no justice because as that woman rightly pointed out, someone ought to have killed the girl. If I am convicted, that is even worse injustice, because then you have failed not only her but also me. I am starting to feel I would rather be convicted. That would at least be my penance for so monumentally failing the girl I love."

"Vishal, unfortunately, you are my client because you hired me to defend you. Between absolving you and serving her justice, the former is my priority and I am bound by duty."

"Then make it your damn priority." He slams the glass of scotch on the table near his elbow as he yells at me with uninhibited fury. I take a step back and try to shield myself from his sudden verbal attack. "Is it about the money? I have access to my grandfather's trust fund. I will sign a cheque right away. It's all yours."

That's hurtful. Nobody has ever questioned my professional integrity before, and this guy standing before me is barely a man, accusing me of dubious intentions.

"It's never about the money. Let me tell you, your father hired me on a fixed-fee basis. I have nothing to gain or lose except my reputation, which I am yet to build in this country."

"It's my father then. It's his mandate. Isn't it? He doesn't have faith in his own flesh and blood, and he has managed to corrupt you too. All he cares about is getting me out. It's not me that matters. It's not my loss that concerns him. I am a liability that he must carry for the sake of his career and his reputation. And I have become exactly that to you as well."

"Vishal …"

"Don't. Don't reason with me. Before I leave, let me remind you, your own words. The truth is out there, and it's absolute and sacrosanct. It's not for comfort. It's for liberation. Good luck, Mr. Bhargav."

He looks over at something behind me in a pointing gesture, nods and leaves. I turn and look up at the object of his message. It's a painting, my father's only gift to me ever, which he gave to me upon my graduation. A painting made by my maternal grandmother and a wedding gift to my father. The painting is trichromatic in black, white and grey colours and depicts a scene. There is a shadow of a man holding a lamp and walking in a dark forest. The flame of the lamp is the only object in white. The man is in the middle of a step and all around him, over the trees, near his feet and far away, there are shadows of various creatures that look scared and are running away from the man's shadow in fear. The man's palm is wrapped around the lamp in a protective gesture, and the flame appears to be flickering a bit. Below the painting is an inscription in my grandmother's beautiful cursive handwriting.

"*Dharmo rakshati rakshitah* (Protect the truth and the truth will protect you)."

I stare at the painting for a long time, willing the anxiety in my heart to settle down. I need to introspect. I drop a quick text to my wife that I need some alone time and walk over to the beach. I keep walking for a long time, trying to find a quiet spot, but there always seems to be someone or the other. This is something about Singapore that I miss. In India, it is difficult to find a secluded spot that is also safe. After a few steps, I find a patch with a couple of lounge chairs facing the sea. I drop myself on one of them, look at the sky and will my thoughts to come clean.

Today's standoff with Vishal was unexpected and, in a sense, shattering. Because I realized I am failing my defendant. In my career so far, I have always managed to keep my clients happy. Most often than not, it's an out-of-court settlement with long-drawn negotiations with the opponents. But I am an excellent negotiator, and I have always managed to save a few pennies or sweeten the deal for my client. You know what they say about lawyers. A lawyer with a briefcase can steal more money than a hundred men with guns.

In this case, too, I always knew where I stood, and yet, I gave it my best. Although my mind always battled with the question of Vishal's innocence, I had managed to push the misleading thoughts to the back and focus on winning instead.

Now, they come out unbidden again. For one, it's clear Vishal cares about the girl because he wouldn't have fought with me to find out the truth. And then there is the question of doing right by the girl. Should I be really concerned about that? Maybe I should, because then it serves both purposes; justice to the girl and justice to my client. But where do I start? Is Vishal really innocent? I go over the case in my mind, starting from the first day I met Vishal at the prison. I scan each and every minute since then, like a picture in slow motion. It comes to a halt at the prosecutor's question that day, "Why would someone kill a simple uncontroversial college girl who has no enemies?"

The question repeats itself over and over again, until I am mentally exhausted. I take a deep breath and call a cab to take me home. My family is asleep, so I tiptoe into my bedroom, slowly lie on the bed and fall into a troubled slumber.

CHAPTER 16

Ajay

I wake up the next day, look at my phone, and realize it's almost noon—way past the breakfast time. There is a missed call from Sanjay, followed by a quick text stating it's not urgent. I feel slightly disoriented, maybe from the wee bit of scotch I had the previous night, so I take a quick shower, put on my shorts and head to the drawing room. My daughter is watching her favourite episode of Peppa Pig, where the grandfather pig is doing some gardening work. She is so fascinated with the cartoon that she doesn't notice me. Tavi is helping my son rehearse a story. I think he is participating in a storytelling competition at a summer camp. She is off-duty today and looks relaxed and peaceful. She gives me a smile as I walk in and gestures towards the food on the table so I can help myself. She and my son are sitting on the other end of the table, and I take a seat across from them. It's nearly lunchtime so I start with a cup of coffee and serve myself a generous portion of the pulao and cottage-cheese gravy spread out in front of me.

I hear their conversation as I eat. It's an Arab folktale about a traveller who rents a donkey and its rider for a long trip in the desert. The trio start early in the day and by noon are exhausted from travelling in the hot sun. The traveller decides to rest and looks for shade around the desert but cannot find any. Meanwhile, the exhausted donkey sits in the sand and its rider walks a bit to look around. The traveller sees the shadow of the donkey and takes a seat near the animal and makes himself comfortable. The rider sees this, approaches the traveller and asks for money for using the donkey's shadow. The traveller argues that since he paid for the donkey, usage of its shadow is included in the price. The rider argues that the price paid was for the donkey alone and not its shadow. They start arguing and after some time, realize that the donkey slipped away when they were immersed in the argument. The moral of the story is that when you get too involved in petty arguments, you lose things that matter.

As my son finishes the narration, I almost choke on my food. Because this sure looks like a cosmic joke on my situation right now. Tavi gives me a perplexed look but doesn't say anything. They continue, and after a while, Arka leaves for his playtime. Aria goes to her bedroom for her noon nap. And now, Tavi and I are alone in the balcony.

The balcony is the best feature of this house and is somewhat close to what we had in Singapore. It's wide and spacious and has my daughter's favourite flowerpots all along the railing. It's on the first floor of the duplex and has a view of the sea on one side and our community pool on the other. Tavi bought a double lounge chair and a small coffee table for this place, making it perfect for a situation like this. We sit on the lounge chair—me with my back against the headrest and legs stretched out, and Tavi snuggled between my legs with her head resting on my chest. My arms are wrapped around her waist, and she is drawing circles on my palm—something she does when she is listening to me intently.

I tell her what happened with Vishal, his outburst and then my dilemma and predicament. She listens to me carefully but stays silent for a few moments. Then, she says, "You know Peter—our neighbour's Peter Jackson, as she lovingly calls him?"

Okay, Peter Jackson needs some introduction. On the first

weekend after we moved here, my mother, Tavi and I were busy unpacking the house. We could not leave the kids at my parents' home because nobody was there to watch over them. My father was around but he is persona non grata. So the little monsters were running all over the place, and we were having a tough time keeping them in check. A friendly old lady, Mrs. Jackson, came to our home asking if we needed anything. She looked around and realized we needed help with the kids.

"Oh! Why don't you send the kids to play at our home? Peter will love their company."

We immediately jumped at the offer and sent the kids along with her, each with one toy. It's parenting rule 101 to always send your kid with a toy of their own when going to a friend's house, because kids are extremely possessive about their stuff. And if the other kid refuses to share their toys, chaos ensues.

When Mrs. Jackson looked at the puppy soft-toy in Aria's hands, she exclaimed, "Peter is going to have such fun!"

After a while, my kids returned home, and I found Aria's soft toy missing. Apparently, Peter had torn it off completely. Aria was quite upset, and I had to console her with a promise to buy her a new one. But I was furious with Mrs. Jackson for being so irresponsible.

"Aria, what was his mother doing at that time?"

"She was watching TV, Daddy."

"Did she not try to intervene when the boy tore up your doll? That's shocking!"

"No Daddy. What could she say? Peter is so young …"

"How old is he?"

"Just one year old."

"What? That's outrageous! How could she just leave her infant son unsupervised, with two kids?"

That's when my son decided to put me out of my misery. "Dad, Peter Jackson is Mrs. Jackson's German Shepard. She treats the puppy like her son."

That's when I realized the world is full of strange and silly people, some of who pass on their last names to their dogs. And that's how Peter Jackson came into our lives. I saw the dog a few days ago. He's a little beast that looks more like a fox than a dog. He loves kids and hates toys. Deadly combination—that one.

I snap out of my reverie when Tavi clears her throat. I am still wondering what Peter Jackson has got to do with my case. "Why are we discussing disruptive canine behaviour?"

"Let me tell you what happened. So Peter Jackson got a vaccine shot or something, but he didn't react well to it. Today, Peter started running amok when Mrs. Jackson brought him for a walk in the community park. Vishal was just entering the lobby when it nearly pounced on him. But he calmed Peter down and managed to keep him under control until Mrs. Jackson could fetch his leash. Peter immediately took a liking to Vishal. He was bouncing up and down and was excited to get his attention."

"Tavi ... What is your point?"

"I believe Vishal is innocent."

"Because a crazy dog likes him?"

"Yes. They say dogs have extrasensory perceptions and can identify dubious or bad people. Besides, Peter Jackson is very sensitive and cautious about strangers. But he got so comfortable with Vishal, and so quickly. I think he is a good man."

I try to absorb what she is saying but cannot wrap my head around it. "Tavi. These two things are not really connected, and they definitely cannot be presented as an argument in the court."

"Remember you talked about experience and perceptions in the court. Well, this is my perception. Besides, it is not far-fetched. There is a scientific basis for it. I have one more theory along these lines. Remember Vishal's friend Sameer mentioned how they used to sing at the bar in the hotel and donate the proceeds to underprivileged children? Those are the actions of a very kind-hearted person. Such a person *killing* an innocent young girl is just unbelievable."

"Maybe his violent tendencies are directed to just young women and this girl in particular."

"That's a bit of a stretch. Sameer also mentioned his autistic younger brother also loved Vishal. All these simply don't add up."

"Okay, let's assume what you are saying is correct. How does that help the case?"

"It's a starting point. A different starting point."

And that's when it strikes me. Maybe I have got it all wrong. It's as if you lose the GPS signal during a drive to an unknown place and suddenly the signal is back on and the map reroutes and shows a different direction altogether. My wife's tangential theories have untangled the lingering thoughts in my head and got me rethinking my view about Vishal's innocence. I have been so absorbed with getting him out that my sole focus has been Vishal and his actions, and I have been pretty much blind to the rest of the situation.

It's a deception that happens to many of us. Let's take a black dot in the centre of a white paper. When the paper is presented to us, the first object of our interest is the small black dot and not the vast expanse of white area around it. Let's hypothetically say the dot is changing in size, most of us would study the varying size of the dot, but not the growing or shrinking white area around it. I am facing a similar situation here. I think deeper and deeper and then that question flashes in my head like a neon light, "Who killed the girl? If not Vishal, who killed the girl?"

I spend the rest of the evening wracking my brain to come up with answers to the question. It is times like this that wish I had more experience in murder mysteries and criminal psychology. I would have had a repertoire of possibilities and theories to pick, apply and eliminate. Now I have to rely solely on my intellect and originality. I can feel a headache looming behind my brows when I see Arka playing with his Lego blocks in our hall. It's one of his favourite Lego 3-in-1 sets. He has already assembled a motorbike, and now, he is disassembling the pieces one by one to start over and build a race car—as shown in the manual. The thing is, the same pieces can be assembled and morphed to build two entirely different structures, but the starting point and the steps are totally different.

As I stare at the blocks in front of me, I remember the details relating to the crime scene, and my brain parses all the information it has collected since the case landed on my desk. A theory slowly takes shape in my head. I develop it internally, step but step, and by the end of it, an entirely new scene presents itself. I swallow hard as I ponder over this outcome. The result is terrifying, and I realize I will need a myriad of resources to prove it. My heart thrums with an adrenaline rush, and I panic not knowing what to do and how to go about it.

As I am pacing the hall in unconcealed agitation, our doorbell chimes. I suddenly stop in my tracks. Tavi opens the door and my jaw drops at the sight of our visitor.

It's my father.

CHAPTER 17

Ajay

My father. The last person I would ever expect to visit our home. Maybe he is here to discuss the case? But he promised not to interfere. So perhaps he wants only a quick update?

Tavi is obviously nonplussed too, because it takes a few moments for her to invite him in. He steps into the house and glances around, slowly taking in his surroundings until his eyes land on Arka playing on the floor. He politely greets his grandfather and asks him to sit down. A few minutes later, Aria runs into the room and beams upon seeing her grandfather.

I feel suffocated. I need to get out of here. I take the stairs to the first floor, walk into my office room, and try to slow down my breaths.

Why is my father here? What do I tell him? I am not ready, and I cannot deal with a confrontation with him. But I have to face him eventually. I am sure Tavi must be doing some damage control by explaining my sudden disappearance. But I cannot keep him waiting for long. I walk over to the refrigerator to pour myself some scotch. As I open the refrigerator, I hear my father's voice, "Ajay!"

I turn to face him. "Father, I am sorry I walked out like that. I was just a little lost."

He gives me an understanding smile. "I know. My sudden visit must have shocked you."

That's an understatement.

"We just did not expect you. That's all."

He walks around a bit. "You have a beautiful house."

"Thank you. We love it too."

He walks over to the shelf containing my football souvenirs. "Do you still play football?"

"Sometimes. Arka loves football too. We watch a lot of tournaments together."

"Hmm."

"I … I cannot discuss the case right now."

He looks a bit offended. "I am not here to talk about the case. I just wanted to check if my son is okay. Your mother told me about your visit yesterday and how upset you were. I wanted to offer any help I can and also talk to you."

This is surprising, but I soften a bit at this uncharacteristic display of parental concern. "Father, I am fine. Nothing I cannot handle."

"I know. You have done so well so far. In your career, with your family. All without my help."

I blink a couple of times. Why is he saying all this? Is everything okay with his health? If something were wrong, my mother would have told me.

"You brought me into this world. You raised me. I owe you everything."

He gives a small laugh. "Look at you. You are consoling me because you think I feel bad about all of this. That you have achieved so much without my help. You may not believe me, but I am actually very, very proud of you. And also, really happy about how you have handled this case so far. I couldn't have done so well myself if I were in your position."

To say I am shocked will be putting it mildly. My father has never ever said such words to me. I have always been the non-conforming disappointment of a son. And so far, in this case, I have hardly gotten anywhere. I stare at him in undisguised surprise.

"Can we go to the balcony to catch some fresh air?"

I merely follow him, not knowing how to respond or react. He takes a seat on the lounge chair and motions for me to sit next to him. We have never been this close physically. I don't remember him ever holding me or sitting close by me. I always thought my mother alone raised me and took care of me. I am a little offended now, because I feel he is doing this out of pity, as if he is comforting a wounded animal. I don't like it one bit. I have a high quotient of pride too. After all, I am my father's son. So I take a seat on the chair opposite to his instead and lean forward, bracing myself for any bitterness he might show. Only, he doesn't. In fact, he looks hurt too, as if upset that I have refused him this small indulgence.

"I don't want to hurt you. Ever. Believe me, this sort of interaction is difficult for me as well. I haven't done this before. But I want to try."

Why does he make it sound like a favour to me? If it's so difficult then why doesn't he end this and make it easier for both of us?

"I am really proud of you. I have been for a very long time. I just didn't know how to show it."

"Father, I am not sure what to say. I have turned out to be someone you never expected. So what you are saying is definitely unbelievable."

"Yes. You are so very different. And that's exactly why I am proud. You know I always looked at our relationship like one of dependence. I would provide for you, and so you were obligated to be what I wanted you to be. I thought that's what fatherhood was about. Because I never had a father figure. I grew up without any love or affection. My foster parents cared for me but not in a parental sort of way. So I grew up with a notion that love was not needed. I became what I am, very driven and very successful, without any love at all. I wanted a child to carry my legacy forward, and when you came into our lives, I made it my responsibility to ensure you lived up to the legacy. Your mother loved you beyond limits, and I thought she loved enough for both of us. So I committed myself to making sure you succeed.

"But all along, I forgot about love and affection and how beautiful and fulfilling they can be. I wanted you to depend on me because that was the only way I could play a role in your life. But as you grew up and became more and more independent and…distant, I realized I had no role to play at all. Look at you. You have become a wonderful man and none of it is because of me."

He stops and swallows, and I think I see restrained tears in his eyes. I want to comfort him, not out of pity, but because he is my father. But I hold myself back. Because for the first time in my entire life, and probably his entire life, he is opening up to me and becoming vulnerable. I am the only person to see this side of him, and I feel humbled at that realization. He quickly composes himself and continues.

"You have done so well in life. I heard about your achievements in Singapore. You are a loving husband and a doting father. Your wife and kids adore you. I was always feared but never loved. I am so very proud of you, Son, and I couldn't be happier that you didn't follow in my footsteps."

"Why now? After all these years, why now?"

"Because I have come to my senses. Because I don't want to fail you anymore and miss out on things in life that really matter. Because despite the fact that I haven't been there for you, you have always been there for me. Because you have tried and tried for so many years, and now, I want to make it happen because only I can make it happen. Because you can put your pride aside and still be my son. You took this case up without a word because your father owes someone else. Because no matter what happens to this case or anything else on the face of this earth, I have always loved you—and will always do."

There are only two instances in my life when I have cried. First, when my son was born, and I held him in my arms. The second, when my daughter was born, and she wrapped her tiny hand around my finger. This is the third. I am speechless with overwhelming emotions. I run my palms over my face to compose myself, take a few moments and speak. "Thank you, Father."

"No thanks to me. It's all you."

"I will always be there for you. I am your son."

"Yes. I couldn't be prouder to be your father. And I wanted to congratulate you on this case as well. You have done so well so far."

"You are just being generous. I haven't gotten anywhere. We have reached a roadblock. I don't know how to go from here."

"Tell me ..."

"I believe Vishal is innocent. But I need time and help to prove it."

"Take me through your thinking."

And I take him through my hypothesis, and he listens to me intently, not countering me or interrupting me on any assumption.

After I am done, he smiles at me.

"That's impressive. And I have just the right man for you on this. He will help you with the time and means to make it happen."

"Who are you talking about?"

"Subbu. Ex-CBI. One hell of a guy. We worked on a case years ago, and it was a terrific experience working with him. We share a mutual respect. He runs his own private investigation agency. It's low-key but one of the best in this city. You need a job done - you need Subbu. I will connect you to him."

"Thank you, Father. I will speak to him and rope him into this case. Sanjay will do the needful paperwork."

"Sure. Now can we please go down and meet the kids? They are so adorable. Aria looks just like your mother. She is beautiful, isn't she?"

"Yes. She is the princess in this house. She is like Mom in most ways. Endearingly stubborn."

"Don't tell me. If not for your mother, I wouldn't have been here. But that's a story for another time."

We walk downstairs to find Tavi arranging the table for five people. She softly asks my father if he would like to stay for dinner.

"Yes, sure. Is that the pasta Aria talked about? I would like to try it, please."

And that's how our evening is spent. My father is contently relaxed as he engages Aria and Arka in a conversation, and he offers to take them out for ice cream. My kids take an immediate liking to their grandfather and are already discussing their weekend plans with him. After the kids get ready for the ice-cream outing, my father looks at me and tells me I am lucky to have found such a good wife.

What a beautiful evening it has been. I realize that unconsciously, I have always been pining for my father's approval. Because deep down, I want to carry on the rich legacy my father had built and settle down in my country where I was born and grew up. I also wanted to take care of my parents, especially my mother. Today, finally, I have his approval, and it soothes my soul like nothing else. I feel jubilant and enervated.

The next day, I call up Subbu, and we agree to meet for breakfast at a nearby restaurant. I asked Tavi for suggestions on a good breakfast place, so that's where we are going. All the thinking, debating and reconciling over the last couple of hours have given me a ginormous appetite, and I think the sight of a delectable buffet spread could soothe my hunger a bit. Tavi suggested this place knowing it is not too far from where we live. *Bhojan* is a rustic restaurant that serves buffets for breakfast, lunch and dinner, and they are known for their diverse blend of breakfast dishes that combine flavours from across the world. I have a feeling Subbu is a foodie and is going to love this place. After I reach the place, I am convinced it's the perfect choice. We could have a good conversation over breakfast, go over the case details and also get to know each other a bit.

I have never dealt with private investigators, and I am not sure how to use their service either. But my father helped me out by discussing all the commercial terms with Subbu and the Mehtas, so that's out of our way. As I wait for my guest with a cup of coffee, I hear someone call out from behind my shoulder. I turn to see a man dressed in a faded, blue shirt and a pair of dark slacks. He would be in his late forties with dark complexion and small eyes. His hair is cut in military style, and a pair of sunglasses are tucked in the top two buttons of his shirt.

I know this is my guest. I stand up and shake hands with him. "Ajay Bhargav."

"Subramanya Shankar. Subbu to you."

"Glad to meet you. My father speaks highly of you."

"Thank you for your kind words."

We take our seats as the waiter serves us some freshly prepared fritters and pours us more coffee, but Subbu politely declines. I give him a questioning look.

"No caffeine. It slows down my thinking."

How strange! I thought caffeine energizes your brain. But I proceed to the business at hand. "Do you know about the case?"

"Broadly. I have been following the news, and your father gave me a lowdown last night. I had a quick conversation with Kishore Mehta this morning."

"The next hearing is in five days. And I am worried that's too short a time."

"Do you have a plan?"

"Yes, I do. But it may need your inputs."

"Take me through it."

"Nope. I should show you for a more convincing pitch."

He looks surprised and stares at me for a few seconds. Maybe he thinks I have it on my phone as a video or an image. He has no idea.

"Interesting. Let's finish breakfast and get going. So, where do we begin?"

"Where it all began."

CHAPTER 18

Ajay

Intox is a quaint club stationed in a three-storey building. It is spread over about 6,000 square feet and has a wide entrance with frisking facilities and security cameras. There is a small enclosure for frisking women guests. Sanjay had a chat with the club owner Toby Fernandez before coming here and Toby claimed that both the entrance and the exit had CCTV cameras. The outside of the building looks to have been painted recently, but there is paintwork still to be done near the entrance and patio area and they look old and worn out. When I first visited the club, that was the first thing I noticed. A mismatch in colours and contours between the adjoining walls and the entrance area. Maybe that's next on Toby's agenda once the dust settles. The entry doors open into a foyer that in turn opens into a wide discotheque area. On one side of the disco is a reasonably large bar and, on another side, a wall containing pictures from the many batches of college students who had partied here. All around the disco area and on the wall, there are posters of old cinema actresses in their seductive poses but overall the bar doesn't look ribald.

The bar area piques my interest because that's the only way out of the club. Behind the bar is a narrow and long hallway that leads to the exit. On one end of this hallway are restrooms and on the other are lockers for safe-keeping things. On the wall adjacent the bar is a narrow staircase that leads to the first floor. Sanjay, Subbu and I take the stairs slowly and grasp the surroundings as we take each step. It's a long cement staircase with steel railings and the staircase is in the area with the poorest lighting in the entire hall. On the first floor, there is a huge balcony that covers part of the disco area, but most of the dance floor is visible if one stands near the balcony railing. This balcony has three adjoining rooms. Two of them are storerooms I think, and the third is an office room.

The office room is where the crime took place. The three of us approach the room and stop for a moment. The door has a see-through glass panel, and we look inside through that and note that only the desk in front is visible. We are carrying the drawings and photographs that Sanjay had obtained from the police. I gesture for Sanjay to open the door, and he slowly turns the knob and the three of us step inside.

We absorb our surroundings, paying utmost attention to detail. Subbu intermittently looks at the papers in his hand, maybe to verify if everything is exactly as in the crime scene. Thankfully, it is. This office room is not very big. About 500 square feet. The door is facing a mahogany desk and behind the desk is a rotating office chair. Behind the chair is a set of windows with drapes that are closed. To the right-hand wall is a couch, one end of it is near the door and the other end is near the desk. The left-hand side is split into two sections. Near the desk is the bathroom and near the entrance door is a smaller sofa with a small coffee table in the front. One end of the sofa is against one of the walls of the bathroom. The entrance door opens to this wall but since the sofa is deeper into the room, it doesn't obstruct the door when open. On the office desk is a pen stand. There is a lamp in the right-hand corner opposite to the entrance door.

Once we are done with the inspection, I turn to Subbu and Sanjay, "I want to try something. It's still a hypothesis at this stage. But this is the only way to prove it right."

"Go on. We are listening."

"I want to enact the crime scene."

"How?"

"Subbu, you are a proxy for the victim, and Sanjay, you are a proxy for Vishal. Both of you stay put over the couch there. When I knock the door, Sanjay will open it in a minute." And I explain the rest of my plan to him. They understand what I am trying to achieve, and we start the enactment. First Subbu and Sanjay settle on the couch. They look awkward for a few moments. This is a little strange and new to me too, but I had run this over in my head a hundred times since yesterday, so I am more prepared and less flustered about going through with it. I walk out of the room and after a few moments, Sanjay gets up and walks into the bathroom and closes the bathroom door. Once I see through the panel that he is inside, I knock. Subbu comes to open it after a minute. Once the door opens, I jump into action, use my hand to muffle his mouth, push him back against the desk and use the pen, a proxy for the scissors to pretend and stab him in the throat, push him on the couch and pretend to open his pants. Then I move to the opposite sofa that's hidden by the bathroom wall. When Sanjay enters and looks at the couch for a few seconds and steps in the room, I tiptoe into the bathroom and close the door silently.

The enactment is over, and we are sitting in the office room and just staring at each other. Sanjay breaks the silence first. "This is mind-blowing." Sanjay is dumbfounded.

Subbu starts with the questions, "So you are essentially saying that someone was watching the couple and killed the girl when Vishal was in the bathroom?"

"Yes. Vishal told me that he had to fumble with the door to open it. That would have given some time to the murderer."

"I don't think it's a coincidence. It must have been premeditated."

"Possible."

"So then how did he escape?"

"Come with me."

I take them both into the bathroom and show them the vent behind the Western toilet. I have the electrician, from my interaction that night, to thank for this insight. There is a metal handle, and the vent opens without any trouble.

"The day of the incident, the building was being painted and that's why you see those ladders installed against the wall. The murderer got out using them."

"This is unbelievable. This is some genius planning. Someone did a really thorough job," Sanjay exclaims.

"Except, only the act is now no more a secret. But the bigger question is who?"

Subbu has been contemplative throughout, and I want to pick his thoughts on this. I turn to face him when he finally speaks, "I think we should go downstairs and talk."

The three of us head to the ground floor and seat ourselves on the chairs near the bar.

"So, tell us what you are thinking."

"Someone followed the couple closely, knew about their plans for the night and grabbed the opportunity to kill the girl when she opened the door and escaped through the bathroom. We are dealing with a smart chap."

"But how did he know about the bathroom vent?" Sanjay asks.

"Maybe he didn't. He just got lucky. Normally most bathroom vents can be opened from the inside using a simple screwdriver, but he must not have been carrying one. Our man must be very observant. He must have noted the ongoing paint job and the make-shift metal railing installed on the outside wall and acted quickly. True, there is a large element of luck to his escaping unnoticed. But he was very smart, nevertheless. The scissors and precision of the stab to target the carotid artery also confirms this. Someone knew the biology quite well to decide that it would surely kill the girl."

"Who could it be? Was he against the girl or Vishal? The girl is just someone next door, but Vishal comes from a reputed influential family."

"I can't say. But you are right. We need time to figure it out."

"The judge is not going to give any extensions without a proper basis. And I am worried that if we bring up this possibility out in the open, it may tip off our target and he may try to escape or meddle with the potential evidence."

Subbu rubs his thumb against his jaw in a contemplative gesture and is silent for several minutes. And then he says, "I think Kishore Mehta can help us. Leave this to me. I will take care of it."

I am not sure what he is going to exactly do, but somehow, I trust him to take care of it. So, I move onto the next item on the agenda.

"And now, about our suspect. I think we should speak to Vishal and understand a bit more about their network."

"Agreed. But what about the girl? How do we know her side of the story?" Sanjay raises a valid point.

"I think we should rely on Vishal's information for now, eliminate the possibilities, and then see where we stand."

"Sounds like a plan."

⁛ ⁛ ⁛

Vishal is sitting on the loveseat facing the coffee table. As I step into the room, he immediately stands up and stares at me for a few seconds. I walk further into the room and stand facing him. He looks really bad—there is a week's old scruff on his face, his eyes are gloomy and red from lack of sleep, he looks paler and thinner and older. It's as if he has aged ten years over the last few days. I remember our last conversation and I suddenly feel sorry for him. It's clear his father is giving him a tough time. After a successful reconciliation with my father, I feel the urge to help this young man out and decide to speak to Kishore Mehta before I leave this place.

"Vishal, we need to talk, and you might actually like me after you hear what I have to say."

"I have always admired you, Ajay, and I am sorry for my behaviour the other day. It was out of line."

I have seen people lose their shit for things much less significant; I can surely cut him some slack. "You are forgiven." And in a bid to lighten our moods, I add, "But you owe me once I get you out of this."

"I owe you even if you don't get me out. But yes, it's a deal."

"You were right the other day. I was heading in the wrong direction. Now we are on the right track. But I will need your help."

"How can I possibly help you?"

We both sit on the sofa facing each other, and I explain the details to him. I know hearing this is really difficult for him, but there is no way I can soften the blow of the revelation.

"Here is what happened that night Vishal. Someone followed you both and saw you going into the room for your little adventure. They

163

saw you heading to the bathroom and knocked on the door. When Nitya opened, he shut her up with a tight hand on her mouth and I think he was wearing gloves or maybe he used a cloth to wipe away his finger prints. He took the scissors from the pen stand and stabbed her throat and hid behind the sofa on the opposite wall till you were in the bathroom. When you came out and rushed to help Nitya, he slipped inside and escaped through the bathroom vent and got down using the railing on the outside wall."

He looks at me with shock plastered all over his face. His eyes are wide, and I notice tears in the corner of his eyes.

I continue, "I believe you. I believe you are innocent. It's not you and the only way it could have happened is this."

He sits there speechless and deathly still, and I am worried he will go into shock, so I move towards him and put my hand on his shoulder gently.

"Please give me a few minutes to collect myself."

As I wait for him to regain his composure, Subbu enters the room. He tells me Sanjay is running some important errands and turns to Vishal. I introduce them to each other, but Vishal doesn't stand up to shake Subbu's hand.

We wait for a few minutes and then he finally responds. "What do you want me to do?"

"Help us find out who did it."

CHAPTER 19

Ajay

"Who are you looking for exactly?"

This is Subbu's forte, so I sit and listen to their conversation intently. I am already impressed with Subbu and am thankful to my father for connecting us. I am more confident now that we will bring out the truth. Subbu pulls out a small notebook and a pen and begins the process.

"We have to get there one step at a time. I can give you some pointers. He must be someone from your college and from computer science batch because you mentioned that only that batch was partying that night."

"What?"

"Very likely, yes. On that night, there were college students, club staff, and the bouncers. I am not very sure about the latter two. But Sanjay has gone to get the CCTV footage from the night and that may throw more light. But for now, we have to assume it is a student from your college."

"Someone from college would risk so much and commit a crime like this?" Not just Vishal, this is quite shocking to me as well.

"Well, you can never really understand or fathom criminal intentions. But I am guessing it was some kind of vendetta against one or both of you."

"Nitya is a normal girl from a normal family. I cannot believe anyone could hold a grudge against her."

"Let's not rule that out completely. But do you think someone would hold a grudge against you?"

As I am listening to this discussion, a possibility strikes me. "Subbu, do you think it could be a vendetta against his father or the family. The Mehtas have a wide reach and reputation."

"Possible, but this act seems to suggest the vendetta is against Vishal or Nitya. There are more sinister ways to harm his father if that's really the motive. We may have to eliminate a few suspects during the process. But I think this should be our starting point."

I nod and Subbu continues, "We are looking for someone from your college, who knows both of you well and is crookedly smart, agile, and quick on his feet. Physically, I think he would be petite or lean."

"What's your reasoning?"

"This guy could think quickly and figure out that the bathroom is a good hideout and then manage to open the vent door and get out. That indicates some sharp brain. But the vent door was not very wide, so someone who could fit in that easily would have a lean body."

"That's way too many people who could fit your description."

"I know. So, let's start with your common friends. But I want you to think aloud as you evaluate each and every individual so that I take notes and catch as many clues as I can."

"Our common friends are my band members. And only Yogi

is from computer science. But he is not academically strong. He is my junior and Nitya's senior. We never had any disagreement. It's unbelievable that he would resort to such a monstrous crime."

"Okay. I am still putting this guy in the list. We will come back to him later. Now, let's start with your other friends from computer science. Just to be clear, the target could be female."

Vishal thinks for some time and comes up with the names and possibilities one after another. He debates and counters himself as he lists the names, and Subbu asks him more questions intermittently.

"Kay was always interested in me, but I never entertained her. But she doesn't meet your crookedly smart condition. She is totally dumb. Amongst the others, there is only Laksh, who is really smart. He is a fixer of sorts and is damn good at repairing things. He is street smart too. But he never had anything against me."

"I am including this guy too. Just remember, it's not just vendetta against you. It could be against Nitya as well."

"But why?"

"I don't know but a possibility is that she never returned his affections and instead chose you. You can never get your head around a criminal mindset."

"Laksh was never close to Nitya."

"You never know because you were not in touch with her for many months in between. You don't know what happened during that time. Besides, she is your junior so there is so much more time that she would have spent with so many different people," I remind Vishal.

"But that's the problem. There so much I don't know about that time."

I turn to Subbu. "Subbu, we may have a bunch of people by the end of this, and you may have to put someone to watch over them to find out if there is anything suspicious or connected to the murder. Do you think it's achievable, given the time constraints?"

Subbu thinks for a few moments. "Let's get the list ready first, then we will strategize."

"All right, I don't have anybody from my friend-circle. Nitya's close friends are Richa and Siya. Richa is from the same colony and is also her classmate. She is a bright student, but I don't know anything more about her."

"Anybody else amongst her friends? We are looking for the same college, same stream."

Vishal ponders for some time and then finally says, "There are some family friends, I think. Jishnu is his name. Same college and her senior by one year. Nitya thought of him as her brother. She stayed over at their place when her mother and brother were out of town. She once mentioned that he was a bookworm and always had his head buried deep in his books. But I don't know anything about him."

"Who can tell us about this guy?"

"Nobody. I don't even know him remotely."

"What did she tell you about him?"

"Nothing much. Just that they are like cousins, and she is like a daughter to his mother. We could spend a lot of time with each other when she stayed over at their place. Apparently, her brother entrusted her with Jishnu, but she said he was too absorbed with his books and never even noticed where she went and what she did."

"Okay. I am including this guy too. Let me talk to my team and see what we can do. Meanwhile, if you remember anything at all, please make sure to contact me immediately. I am available round the clock. This is my card."

Vishal takes the card from Subbu, and they shake hands. Subbu has to go back to his office to set things into motion, and we decide to meet at my office later. I am left alone with Vishal. This discussion and the revelations must be very difficult for him, because he is now even more worried and anxious than before.

"We have a long list. Do we have that kind of time? The next hearing is a week from now."

"I know. Subbu spoke to your father, and I think he will make it happen."

"My father? I don't think he wants to help me at all. He has given up on me."

"I know you both have issues. But trust me, he is not as selfish as you think, especially when it comes to you. Don't worry, he will come around. I am telling you this from experience."

And what an experience it has been. But Vishal doesn't seem convinced. He just looks around and shakes his head. I want to distract him and take his mind off this hell of an ordeal. I eye the iPod lying on the coffee table.

"What were you listening to? Care to share the name of the balm?"

"*One Last Time* by Vaults."

"Beautiful violin and beautiful lyrics. But is it not too ominous for the present situation?"

At that, he snorts and shakes his head at my obvious attempt to humour him. "You love music too?"

"Very much. My first love."

"And your once in a lifetime love?" He sounds curious about my personal life. Most people think I am a low EQ, Rolex- and Armani-clad corporate robot with little or no personal life. They hardly know the reality.

"I am happily married with two young children."

He raises his eyebrows in surprise and cocks his head to one side. I smile at his presumption.

"Yeah. Now, if you will excuse me, I have to meet your father."

"Thank you very much. See you soon."

⁓ ⁓ ⁓

Kishore Mehta is sitting in his office with a glass of whiskey or some darker spirit, I can't say, and immediately stands up when I enter as if I have interrupted something private.

"Is it a bad time?"

"No of course not. I was just musing."

"Did Subbu explain our plan and constraints to you?"

"Yes. He did. Not to worry. It will be taken care of."

"Mr. Mehta, your son is showing remarkable courage in this most difficult situation, and I feel the need to help him now more than ever."

"I know. He is a brave boy."

"Do you really know?"

He looks at me with a frown marring his face as if I am being nonsensical, by insinuating that he doesn't know about his own son's well-being.

"I am nobody to give you parental advice, but please don't deprive him of your support and understanding. I know it's difficult for you to empathize with young love and approve his relationship with the girl, but your son really loved her and is struggling to deal with her loss."

"I care about my son, Ajay. Never doubt that. My earlier reactions were a manifestation of my fatherly insecurities. But deep down, I know we raised him well. At least his mother did. And I am happy that you have something hopeful for us."

"Vishal is crushed but trying to be sane for the sake of the girl. He believes you don't want to help him. He has lost hope, Mr. Mehta. And that's a loss of a lifeline. Forgive me if I am out of line for saying this. God help me, while I can save your son's life, I cannot save *him*. That's all in your hands."

"Oh God! Why does he think so badly of me? And no, you are not out of line. Your father is the closest to a brother I never had. You are family to me. Thank you for telling me this."

"No problem. We will update you once we make some progress."

"Sure." I get up to leave and carry on my business when I hear him say, "Your father called me yesterday. He is so proud of you."

My face breaks into a huge grin at his words. I give him a small nod and head back to my office.

CHAPTER 20

Ajay

The next day, I head to my office to meet up with Subbu and Sanjay. I offered to meet Subbu at his office, but he insisted on meeting us here, saying the space is better here. I think he is like the proverbial Sherlock Holmes who works out of small offices in dingy places. When I reach our conference room, he is already sitting there waiting for me. Sanjay texted me earlier that he would be a few minutes late but that we should start the meeting without him. I enter the conference room and greet him.

"Hey. Can I get you something to drink?"

"Some water."

"Coffee or tea?"

"Just water."

"Oh! Right. I remember, no caffeine. So, about yesterday's meeting with Kishore. Is everything in order?"

"Yes. He is going to take care of it. Quite a man he is."

"You will be glad to be a part of this case, if you have admired him as an actor. You can get some coverage too."

"Oh no! I am not his fan. And no coverage either; I really value my privacy."

I laugh internally. What an absurd thing coming from a private detective who makes a living out of peeping into other people's private lives.

"Whatever is being done to postpone the hearing, may I know if it's within the law and not some hanky-panky?"

He cocks his head to a side and stares at me for a couple of minutes. "Let's just say nobody would think that the hanky-panky being done is illegal. But if we still need more time, we may need your father's help."

His answer is evasive, but I'd rather not know any further. "How could my father help?"

"Your father and the public prosecutor are contemporaries. She may listen to him out of respect. If you both request, the date may get extended."

"So, why not speak to my father first?"

"Because if she refuses and *then* we have to resort to hanky-panky, she may suspect our involvement and that will put us in trouble. Besides, by that time, I am hoping we make some progress that would convince her to give it a chance. Don't worry. It's all good."

"If you say so. Now coming to the list. There is this girl, Amrita, who is Vishal's friend. They had a brief affair when he was in London. Somehow, she gives me jitters. I think you should look into that too."

"If she was involved, whoever she used to get the job done must have been in the bar that day. I think the CCTV footage will throw some light."

"Sanjay will be here with the feeds."

Sanjay had spoken to Toby and DCP Raghuram before coming here and they gave him some pointers. When he joins us in the conference room, he opens the relevant files and turns to us before starting the stream. "A couple of things to note from my discussions today. Subbu, I got clarity on all the things you were looking for. First, all bar employees and bouncers are required to tag their employee ID cards at the automated security system. All the employees who were on duty that day tagged their ID cards. So, no gaps there. Next, the college students were required to show their ID cards at the entrance before entering the club and any duffel bags they were carrying were manually checked. Lastly, after the crime was discovered, the entire club was evacuated from the entrance, and the exit door was not used. So only those who left the club before the crime scene used the exit door."

With that, Sanjay turns on the video stream. The video feed starts at around 6 p.m. There are a lot of people coming in, and a few of them are in chef and waiter uniforms. At around 8 p.m., students start to pour in. Mostly, only the girls are carrying bags. Some men have bags too, but there seems to be nothing unusual about the contents because the security personnel let them pass without any issues. At around 9 p.m., we see Vishal enter with his friends, and a while later, Nitya enters along with her friend. She appears happy and excited as she steps into the club. After around 10.30 p.m., we see Vishal and Nitya dancing with each other. It's not a continuous feed because there are around four CCTV cameras surveying the dance floor and there are some blind spots, but this is what we have. There are few guys sitting by the tables and nothing seems unusual. Unfortunately, none of the cameras reach as far as the stairwell so we don't see Vishal and Nitya going upstairs, we only see them walking towards that wall. A while later, there is scrambling and we see a few guys running towards that side and then sometime later, the entire crowd is seen exiting the club through the entrance door. The exit security cameras don't show anything out of place. There are about twenty people who must have left before the incident. Subbu takes screenshots of the people to check with Toby and Vishal and validate their identities. We are going with elimination here.

The CCTV footage gets us nowhere, and I am a little disappointed. I know it's too early to expect clues, but I was hoping for *some* progress from where we stood in the morning. Subbu takes the screenshots to discuss with Vishal.

Later in the evening, I am on my way to my parents' home to check on my father's health and give him a quick update on the case. Chainsmokers' *Don't Let Me Down* is playing on the car stereo. It's too heavy on treble and too loud and not exactly my kind of music, but somehow, the displaced beats are an effective distraction from the disappointment I am feeling. I am still driving when I get a call from another partner at our firm. He tells me about a money-laundering case that they are working on and requests me to join the team formally. I love that kind of work and want to take up the case but have to decline. I just started here, and this case is taking up all my time.

Earlier in the day, Tavi sent me a text about their plans to have dinner at my parents' place. And now, I am heading there to pick them up and also meet my father. I feel closer to him now more than ever. When I enter my parents' home, I am surprised by the sight that greets me. A beaming Arya is sitting on my father's lap and reading him a story. He is placing soft kisses on her head, and there is a look of utter bliss on his face as he watches his granddaughter talk animatedly about something in the book. Arka is lying on my father's reclining chair and his eyes are glued to the TV. That reminds me that there is a football tournament today—Manchester vs Chelsea—and I am sure that's what is keeping my son occupied.

I step into the drawing room to greet everyone. My daughter is the first to see me, and she gets off my father's lap and runs to me excitedly. I catch her, pick her up in my arms, and give her a bear hug. My father sees me and gives me a happy smile. As I put Aria down, my wife comes up to me and tells me she has some happy news to share. She got hired as a visiting consultant at the community hospital near our home, the one where we met for the first time. I give her a quick kiss on her head. I know my parents are not used to such a display of familial love, but that's how Tavi and I have been for years. It comes naturally to me, and I never want to change our lifestyle. But thankfully, my father doesn't express any irritation at the scene playing out in front of him. My son is too absorbed to greet me, so I go over to him and ruffle his hair. He looks exactly like his mum and is like her in so many ways. He swats my hand away in frustration. Manchester, his favourite team, must not be playing well.

We finish up dinner over an easy conversation, and my father engages the kids with questions about their new school. Despite the anxiety about the case that's eating at me, I feel at peace.

After dinner, I head to my father's library, where he usually sits for a while after dinner and reads a bit. He smiles at me warmly, and I take a seat near him on the sofa.

"You spoke to Kishore Mehta this morning?" I ask.

"Yes. I did. Wanted to assure him that everything is going to be fine."

"He is being too hard on his son. That chap is spiralling."

"How do you know? Did he meet you?"

"Yes. The day before you came to visit us at our home. He was furious, restless, and desperate. Actually, I started thinking about this differently only after our standoff. That and Tavishi's theory."

"Tavishi's theory?"

"You will laugh about it. But yeah."

"Quite a woman she is, that wife of yours."

"I couldn't agree more."

"Subbu spoke to me as well. I didn't want to know any details. Don't want to stress myself at this age and with this health. But overall, I get the feeling that you people are on the right track."

"I hope so, Father. But you never know. We are up against someone really smart here."

"Ajay, there is some advice I would like to give you."

"Yes, please."

"Once you and Subbu have the evidence and arguments ready, you will have to plan your defence at the next hearing very carefully. I suggest that you bring the case to a closure in a single session. This judge has a penchant for long hours at a single stretch. Use that to your advantage. When the time comes, I will pull a couple of strings to avoid multiple hearings."

"I get it. But why are you saying this?"

"This is a high-profile case and however inhuman and blunt it may sound, media and these human-rights groups find Vishal's conviction more entertaining than anything else happening in our society at present. If you delay the case any further, their interference may cause problems."

There is one thing that my father taught me himself and that is chess. I am quite good at it and what's important in chess is to think five moves ahead. Practising law is in a way similar. You have to guess your opponent's arguments and line of thinking five steps ahead.

"I will keep that in mind. That's some useful advice."

"One more thing. But not connected to the case."

"Whatever it is, don't hesitate to ask."

"Can you both think about moving to our home? I know it's too early and all of us need to get more comfortable with each other. But will you think about it?"

And that is when I know that my father is feeling lonely and really wants to connect with us.

"Sure, Father. We will think about it."

CHAPTER 21

Ajay

Over the next two days, I am working on structuring my arguments and planning my defence with the limited information I have. Subbu has put his chaps on the list of people we have zeroed down on. But I know deep down that we could go horribly wrong using our present approach, and we don't have a plan B either. I am anxious and restless for any positive news, and that is when I get a call from Sanjay.

"Hi, Sanjay! What's the news?"

"Actually, something good. Tara has applied for a ten-day leave starting today. A family emergency, apparently, and she has requested for the High Court to postpone the hearing by a week. Just got an official correspondence from the court. That gives us a week more."

"That's awesome. I am assuming Mr. Mehta has something to do with this?"

"Yes. I think so."

"Sanjay, what's the family emergency? Have we gone too far?"

"I don't know. But Subbu might know something. He too has got something for us. He wants to meet us at our office in an hour. But Ajay, I have to head to Delhi for a critical meeting. I won't be back till this weekend. I have left the necessary papers with your secretary and Sekhar; my team member will help you with the additional paperwork. I am sorry about the sudden change."

"Not to worry. You carry on. Subbu and I will deal with this."

Subbu joins in a while, looking solemn, and takes a seat without greeting me first. I think he definitely has something important for us, although I am not sure if it's good or bad. I notice that he drinks a lot of water during the day, so this time, there is a bottle of cool water ready on the table for him. He eyes the bottle and takes a long swig. After he settles down, I ask him, "Tara requested for the hearing to be postponed."

"That's great news, isn't it?"

"Yes. Except, the reason is a family emergency."

"Okay."

"Is everyone in her family all right?"

"How would I know?"

"Don't play coy, Subbu. It suits neither you nor your profession."

At that, he lets out a huff and cocks his head. I think he does that often, whenever he is assessing someone.

"Her father, who lives in Varanasi, got himself tangled in a petty dispute after doing some underhanded things. We used that to our advantage."

Thank God. That's not bad. I think Subbu knows I am not comfortable with these things. My father would have told him about me, because this guy seems well prepared to handle me.

"Shall we move on to more important things, now that I have put your worries to rest?"

"Yes. Go on, please."

"The CCTV footage. We did some extensive ID-matching from the feeds we have. We are mostly certain that the target is a college student."

"What? A college student from a reputed institution doing something like this is shocking!" I am still unable to fully digest this possibility.

"But it's true. Because Toby clearly says all his employees were around on the ground floor during that time. And he could identify all of them during the emergency evacuation."

"Do you think it's possible that this guy got out of the office room through its entrance door and came down and mingled with the crowd?"

"I don't think so. For one, there is only one way out of the first floor, and that's through this one stairwell. And then his clothes would have carried some bloodstains, and he would have been easily caught. Or he would have been caught when Toby's team rushed upstairs when Vishal called for help. As you rightly theorized, he must have used the bathroom door. Vishal claimed that he had to fumble with the door. I think this guy bolted the door partially from the outside, pushed Nitya to the couch, and then hid behind the sofa. Then he tiptoed and escaped into the bathroom. That's the only way to explain the chain of events."

"That means whoever did it could not have used the entrance or the exit. So, we are left with someone from their college. You are right."

"Yes. My boys have come back with some information. First is about this girl, Kay. She is not who we are looking for. Vishal identified her in the evacuation video feeds. Besides, my boy tells me the girl is an out-and-out socialite. She loves galas and parties and all the jazz, and has her eyes set on becoming a model. It's not her."

"There is this guy, Yogi. Vishal cannot tell if he was in the evacuation feed. But my boy says he has a serious girlfriend, and they have been together for over a year now. I think she is his classmate. The video feed showed the girl walking out of the club with a boy on her arm. We figured out who she was and investigated a bit. So, he is out too for now."

"Your folks figured out who the girlfriend is and then connected the dots? That's some impressive work."

"Thanks.
How about someone entering the club from another opening?".

"Yes. We scanned the entire club today. No chance of entry from anywhere else. The club workers confirmed that they cleaned all the three rooms that were upstairs just before the party started. So, he couldn't have been there at that time. Also, our chap should have been watching the couple's movements, according to your theory. I doubt any other hideout is possible."

"Okay, so then what about these two remaining chaps, Laksh and Jishnu?"

"That's the challenge. Neither of them could be identified in the feeds. And both of them meet our criteria. Laksh is Nitya's classmate and was known to be friendly with the girl. Really brainy guy. He won the Android smart app challenge this year. He has a lean frame. No other romantic pursuits. He is now studying to go abroad for higher studies. Then there is Jishnu. Her senior from the same stream, who also lives in the same colony. Quiet guy. His mother and Nitya's mother are co-workers at the garment company. He is also thin and short. Very hard-working and sincere. Does petty jobs to help his mother pay their bills."

"So you are focused on these two people now? How long do you think it's going to take?"

"I don't know. But in my experience, I think there should be a trigger for their true nature to come out."

"What does that mean?"

"Look, most criminals would go on with their lives normally to avoid suspicion. And unless there is some event or information that threatens their incognito status, they won't indulge in suspicious behaviour."

"So you plan to create a trigger to monitor their response?"

"Yes. But I need to watch them more closely to do anything."

"Understood. I am only worried about time."

"There is something else too. I went to the DCP and got hold of the girl's belongings. Looks like she bought an emergency contraceptive and carried it in her purse to the party."

"What? How did the police miss this?"

"They found it but didn't suspect anything. The pill was kept loosely without its plastic packaging or the strip. Thankfully they kept the contents, and I sent it for testing. The lab figured out what it was."

"Hmm ... this corroborates Vishal's account of things."

"How?"

"He told me he was open about his desires to Nitya. She is an educated girl, so she must have done some research on contraception and bought the pill as a precaution."

"Oh. Okay. That makes sense. There is one last thing. This is important. The metal makeshift railing installed against the outside wall. We found some bloodstains on one of the steps where the corner is sharp. I think the murderer injured himself while climbing down in haste."

"Have you given those samples for testing? Can we do a DNA match?"

"I don't think that's possible. It's been too long. They can only confirm that it's human blood, but it cannot be matched with anyone's DNA."

"Then how is it useful?"

"Our suspect has an injury on his legs. Maybe in the lower end of his calf muscle."

"Subbu, what's your hunch?"

"I don't have one, Ajay. And I am refraining from guessing as that may skew my view of things. But I must say, the chap had some fantastic luck on his side to have escaped like that."

"There is one more problem. If our evidence is not direct but only circumstantial, then we are back to square one. It's difficult to acquit based on circumstantial evidence. This court may exonerate Vishal, but there is a high chance of an appeal with the Supreme Court or the CBI. That will be even more hellish than the current situation."

"I know. We will try not to push it that far."

With this new piece of information about a possible injury during the descent using the stairwell, I am more hopeful that we will be able to narrow down on something soon, especially since Subbu's boys are doing thorough fieldwork.

❖ ❖ ❖

Later that day, I check with Vishal on the pill that Nitya had been carrying. He tells me that during one of their conversations, they had discussed these private details, and he had asked her to Google the possible options. This further reinstated my faith in him. He was surely a responsible young man and was not looking to take advantage of an innocent girl.

While I wait for Subbu to come back with more information, I decide to oversee the administrative aspects of my firm. I'm pleased to find that our collections are good and receivables, sound. During my time with Lawson in Singapore, I was assigned the position of chief finance controller and was responsible for overseeing our accounts from time to time. While the systems here are very different, the finance and admin teams are fairly efficient. I am starting to get the hang of working here, and though I miss my corporate life in Singapore, I am getting used to this place as well.

CHAPTER 22

Ajay

It has been more than twenty-four hours since I have heard from Subbu. I did not want to come across as a pestering client by calling and checking repeatedly, so I stayed put although my fingers itched to call or text him. I am sitting in my office, going through the latest developments in cyber-security laws when my phone rings with Subbu's incoming call. I pick up before the second ring.

"Looks like someone missed me."

"Good afternoon to you too, Subbu. Cut the sarcasm and tell me what you have got."

Subbu and I spent some time together yesterday and established a good rapport. He fondly reminisced about his time working with my father and how intellectually stimulating those cases had been. He is eternally grateful to my father for landing him his first client and has the utmost respect for my father's expertise in law. He also told me some clichés about the Indian legal system, and I realized I would benefit a lot from our professional association. We don't have much in common, except that he too, like Tavi, is an ardent follower of Sadhguru. Thanks to our easy conversation yesterday, we now share an enjoyable camaraderie.

"Can you meet me at my office? I will text you the address."

"I thought you liked the space here better."

"Yeah, but work calls. You need to meet my team for this. Come over as soon as you can."

When I give the address to my driver, he is a little sceptical about finding a parking slot there. These days, I am avoiding Uber because the drivers are all but excited to talk to me about the case and grab some gossip. I tell my driver to park it where possible, and I will walk from that point. As I approach Subbu's place, the tall concrete structures slowly start to disappear to be replaced by old, one- and two-storey buildings with no glass but a balcony. The LED streetlights no more adorn the streets. Instead, it is the old long-arm streetlights with rolls of cable wire hanging from them. There are many people who would have lived for decades in the city but wouldn't have seen even one-tenth of it. Well, I am one of them. Coming from an affluent family, I haven't seen anything but the downtown city. After about an hour of efficient driving and a wait at a railway crossing, the cab comes to a halt near a three-storey shopping centre. I get out of the car and walk to Subbu's office, which is ten minutes away.

As my feet carry me through the narrow lanes and alleys with local stores selling all kinds of merchandise, I take a moment to thank Google. Because the navigation seems to work here perfectly. What an effort it would have been to catalogue and tag these streets. Not a single shop seems architecturally correct. Either the front porch is jutting into the street or the balcony is oddly shaped or the paint is clumsy, or the nameplate is rusty. And they sell almost everything. I chance on a store that says they sell AI-enabled toys. Oh! Wouldn't my son love this? Maybe I should bring him here after this case is over.

Finally, I am directed to a slightly wider lane. It's shorter and has a dead end. There are only two buildings on each side. Subbu gave me the name of a salon as a landmark; his office is right opposite the building. I enter the lane and look to my right. There is an air-conditioned hair salon with the picture of Lord Shiva and Parvati sharing half of the same body. The unmistakable feature is their long tresses. The salon is called "Jat-aayu" and its branding is complete with a catchy punchline: *Long Live Your Hair.* I laugh at the whole thing. God! India is such an entertaining and interesting place.

I take the stairs of the opposite building and open the only office door on the floor. There is a visitor's room and another door that is all black and, I think, automated. There seems to be a biometric scanner and a facial-recognition system. When I go there and show my face to the camera, it approves my entry and the doors open, leading me to a larger hall where Subbu is sitting at a round table with two young men. The place is surprisingly contemporary, despite its location. It looks more like a conference room of a small forensic research laboratory. Subbu stands up to greet me and offers me a seat.

"Hello, Ajay! Have a seat. So, how was the experience, driving from Manhattan to Morocco?"

I laugh. "Nice office, Subbu. The salon opposite gave me quite a hearty welcome. I had a good laugh looking at its name board."

"The people are interesting too. You could get a haircut there. It will be fun."

"Will keep that in mind."

"I have some coffee for you. We got it from the tea stall across the street. I've heard they make amazing coffee. Do you want to give it a try?"

"A small cup, please, and thanks for the effort."

I pour myself a cup and take a sip. It's refreshingly different, made using a percolator, I am sure.

"I have some leads for you."

"Tell me."

"I think we may have our guy."

I freeze midway a sip.

"This is my best man, Anjul. He is better placed to explain the situation."

"So, I have been watching Jishnu for a while now," Anjul says. "He is a regular guy, who goes to college and does some petty jobs to make some additional cash to support his mother. He is very hardworking and absorbed with his books whenever he is at home. We did a background check on him. His father was a drunkard and was very abusive towards Jishnu and his mother right from his childhood. I think the father was involved with, uh, prostitutes. He died of STD a few years ago, and Jishnu's mother started working at the Jaipur Garment factory for a living.

"His mother and Nitya's mother are very close friends. Jishnu's mother, Devi, considered Nitya as her daughter, and she has been very sad after her death. After knowing about his background, I started watching Jishnu a bit more closely and also deployed a few more informants. I came to know that yesterday evening, he got into a fight with his mother. Apparently, his mother was feeling distraught about Nitya's death and how she misses the girl's frequent visits. She was feeling upset that the case got postponed further. Jishnu appeared shocked at the news and started cursing Vishal and wealthy people in general. I don't know the exact conversation, but when she talked about Nitya being innocent, Jishnu blew up suddenly, arguing that Nitya was not as innocent as she appeared. That she was a foolish gold-digger and had paid the price for her mistakes. He was really furious and uncontrollable.

"But the more shocking thing is that this is not the first episode where the mother-son duo had a disagreement over the girl's death. His mother thinks his sudden demoralization of Nitya's character is his way of dealing with her loss. She tries to pacify him as best as she can."

I am speechless at this information. This guy surely is our target. I feel a sudden rush of excitement at this development, but I know we still have work ahead of us.

"This is some amazing work, Subbu. Well done, Anjul!"

"Thank you, Sir. I have more actually."

My ears perk up.

"We dug a bit deeper into the family. About four years ago, Jishnu's mother had been working with a plastics company as a cleaning person. She accidentally damaged some goods and earned her supervisor's ire, who fired her immediately. The mother came home crying that day and the next day, the supervisor was found beaten up on the roadside. He knew it was Jishnu, but he refused to file any complaint fearing his family's safety. He moved out of the city immediately, and Jishnu got away with it very easily. His mother is aware of his violent tendencies, maybe knows they are inherited from his father, but tries to comfort him and cover up his actions as best as she can.

"Nitya was like a daughter who often visited their home and spent a lot of time with Jishnu. There is not much evidence of his feelings for her. Everyone thinks they are like siblings or cousins. But despite their closeness, he did not attend her funeral and was absent during the last rites. Again, everyone thought he was just too broken over her loss and overlooked his absence."

I turn my attention to Subbu. "So, you are essentially saying that we have a guy who could possibly be interested in her and is surely close to her. And now he is behaving strangely after her death instead of mourning her."

"Pretty much, yes."

"That's a good start. But we need to develop this further."

"That's what I am planning on. I think we also need to confirm the injury part."

"Subbu, I have a suggestion. Why don't we run this past Vishal and see if he has to add anything? In the light of what happened?"

"That can be done. But I am worried that he will act by himself and that will destroy this case completely."

"Leave it to me. I will convince him. In the meanwhile, figure out a way to confirm the injury."

"Actually, we do have an idea. But we need some help."

"What kind?"

"A doctor. Someone who can do a bit of not-so-legal things for us?"

"What?"

"Don't worry, it's not some wrong prescription or some shady stuff like that. We just need a doctor to ask a few questions for us and allow us to overhear the conversation. And if required, testify in the court."

"Doctors are very reserved people. They won't get out of line so easily."

"Which is why I am asking you."

I hesitate. "You know about my wife …"

He nods. Tavishi may agree if I convince her, but I doubt if she can help. She currently works at a private hospital and getting this guy there will be impossible. Maybe she can connect me to someone. Then it strikes me that my brother-in-law is interning at a hospital near Trombay. Maybe I could speak to him.

"I will try, Subbu. But if it doesn't work, we may have to look for another option."

"That's all I want. We will stay connected on the phone."

✤ ✤ ✤

I meet Vishal at his residence. He is in deep preparation for his upcoming exams. The first exam is the day after the new hearing date. That's why making sure we close this in one hearing is all the more important. Otherwise, I am not sure if he will even scrape through. When I called him today, he sounded hopeful for the first time since I met him. Even now, he stands up immediately when I enter their office room and greets me with a hopeful smile.

"Thank you for rooting for me, you know, by speaking to my father," he says.

"Hey, no problem. I hope you two patched things up."

"I don't know. But he is being polite with me at least."

"That's good. A good first step."

"Yeah. Do you have anything for me?"

"Actually, yes. But I want you to promise me something."

"Promise you what?"

"That no matter what I tell you today, you will not take justice into your own hands and do something stupid to ensure your death warrant. Promise me that you will trust me to do the right thing, that you will not act at all."

"You found him … didn't you?" He swallows and closes his fist tightly as he speaks. I know the cogs in his head are turning at top speed.

"I am not saying anything until you promise me. And I hope you are a man of your word."

He takes a deep calming breath and flexes his palms and gives me an assuring nod.

"Yes. I promise. You can trust me on this."

"We have a lead. It could be Jishnu."

"What?"

"Yes. But we want to confirm it."

"How do you know?"

I tell him about the team's findings and how we need to be sure before we pursue this thread.

Vishal listens carefully without interrupting me and then he finally says, "Nitya never told me anything bad about him. This is utterly shocking. Unbelievable."

"But it may be true. Subbu thinks he exhibits tendencies resembling a split-personality disorder, and his behaviour is definitely suspicious."

"You guys can't be sure that he had feelings for her. Then what else is the motive? We surely never interacted in our lives, and there is no way he has something against me."

"Coming to the first. I want you to remember your conversations with Nitya and tell me anything she told you, that *now* makes sense, in the light of this new information about Jishnu."

Vishal paces the hall in quick steps and is quiet for some time.

"Remember the time when she was staying with their family because hers was away. Anything from that?"

He doesn't say anything and continues pacing. Then suddenly, he stops and turns to me. "They used to have snacks or dinner near the beach on the way to their home. She mentioned some kind of a quiet spot there from where they could have a good view. I think they did that every Thursday, because there is some offer at that eatery."

"Are you suggesting that we speak to the eatery guys, and they can throw some light on how they were being with each other?"

"Yes. Because frankly, she never talked to me about him."

"Did she tell you anything about her other friends or families?"

"Yes, every now and then."

"Okay." I am not sure why this guy was specifically excluded from her conversations with Vishal, and I don't know what to make of it.

"I did once express my reservations about her staying with this guy, but she brushed it off saying he was like a brother."

"Okay. That's what everyone keeps saying. And that's the thing bothering me."

"What do you mean?"

"I am saying we don't have the complete picture. Let me tell Subbu about this eatery and see what he thinks."

❖ ❖ ❖

Later that night, I speak to Subbu and he agrees to dig some information about our target from that eatery. I toss and turn in my bed, restless, because I know all this will not be enough. It will be struck down as scanty circumstantial evidence. We need something big. I know what it is, but I just don't know how to get it. As is the case with all the nights since my return to India, I take a Melatonin pill and force myself to sleep.

CHAPTER 23

Ajay

Early the next day, I call up my brother-in-law to check if he can help. He is a typical doctor right to the bones, bookish and solemn, quite unlike his sister. They don't even look like siblings. Actually, when I met Tavi's family all those years ago, I was completely taken aback. Because she had no resemblance to any of them. It was only when I saw the portrait of Tavi's paternal grandmother that I believed this was truly her family.

Ritesh, my brother-in-law, did not like me much for a very long time after the marriage. He felt I somehow stumped his guileless, good-hearted sister and deprived her of chances to marry a successful doctor. It was only when he saw me during one of his visits to Singapore that he was convinced I was not a bad guy. Since then, we have been on good terms. I am not sure about the future though. Especially after this conversation. But I have no choice because he is the only doctor in this city besides my wife that I know well enough to ask this favour from. And he works at a hospital at Trombay. I don't have many doctor friends. I have always found it difficult to strike a conversation with doctors. The pressures of their education and profession may be the reason, but they don't typically know much about anything other than medicine. The only common topics between us seem to be health, food, and travel. They don't prefer the first one—fed up with that at their job. I am worried about discussing the other two lest they should spoil my passion by giving a hazard warning. Thankfully, I have family to discuss with my brother-in-law, so we surely have something interesting in common.

Ritesh suggests we meet up at the cafe in the hospital. It's been some time since I saw him, and he looks good but much older than I remember. He is five years younger than my wife but is not married yet. My wife says he is too busy with his career and doesn't have time to find Mrs. Right. Well, God save him. Because if he delays it any further, he will become Mr. Wrong to every woman.

We greet each other, and he orders coffee for both of us.

"So, what's up? You know I was a little worried when you wanted to meet me. Is everything okay?"

"Everything is absolutely fine. Your sister is doing great, and she is well and happy. You don't have to worry about anything on that front."

"Haha. So why are we here then? Has it got something to do with the case you are working on?"

"You know about it?"

"Of course I know. Why do you think I wouldn't?"

"Because I didn't think you would follow the news." Remember the theory I had about doctors?

"Oh. That. Actually, I did not come to know through the news. Some staff was talking about the case during a lunch break, and I eavesdropped on the conversation. I have a feeling you are here because of that case. I am right, aren't I?"

My brother-in-law could be very observant when he is not totally oblivious, unlike the typical doctor that he is.

"As a matter of fact, yes. I need your help."

"There is no way in hell that I can help you with shady stuff like that."

"Ritesh, be a little more empathetic. We are talking about an innocent life."

"No, we are talking about sex and alcohol and murder and litigation. All that freaks me out."

"Listen, don't worry. I don't need your help directly. I just need you to connect me to someone who can."

I explain my situation to Ritesh, and he considers this for a while before scribbling the contact details of a doctor who could help. I thank him and we go about our business.

⁂

I call up Subbu and tell him about the eatery Vishal mentioned. He agrees to get some info from the eatery. The thing is, getting information about Nitya is extremely difficult, thanks to the media frenzy. Subbu told me there is a risk of people becoming very curt and unwilling to share any information if she is involved—either for the fear that they may get entangled in a murder case or for the concern that someone is trying to defame her and get Vishal acquitted and deprive her of the justice she deserves. But until now, nobody suspects Jishnu. He is just a regular guy from across the street, so it's easy to fetch some details about him. I am hoping Subbu can figure out something from this eatery.

Subbu and I agree to meet up at Vivek Hospitals near Trombay, where our dubious doctor practises. The hospital is small and looks a little old but is crowded with people, mostly from the neighbourhood,

I think. We ask for Mr. Puri and are led to a small cabin. This guy is a general physician, who has been a consultant at this hospital for over two decades now and is two months away from retirement.

Mr. Puri is a short stout old man with a bald head, a patch of white hair around the ears, a protruding belly, and spectacles clasped to a chain around his neck. He reminds me of Professor Calculus from the Tintin comics. He is wearing a suit and Oxford shoes and an Omega watch. Hmm. That explains why Ritesh connected me to this guy.

Subbu and I look less expensive in comparison. These days I have ditched my Ralph Lauren dress shirts and Louis Vuitton shoes for a plain-looking button-down shirt, and slacks and boots. Subbu always is in an informal attire and wears a Samsung Gear on his wrist. He also carries Bose SoundSport waterproof earphones, the best of their kind. I like his penchant for hi-tech gadgets. He told me he spends a lot of time evaluating and buying them.

When we enter the cabin, Dr. Puri smiles at us and motions to the seats opposite to him. He looks totally free and relaxed, and there are no patients waiting for him at the lobby.

"Hello, Dr. Puri. I am Ajay, and this is my friend, Subbu. Ritesh must have spoken to you about our visit."

"Yes, yes. He did. You are the famous lawyer on the Mehta case, huh?"

"Yes, Doctor. We need some help from you."

"Tell me. People come to me with all kinds of requirements, so please don't hesitate. And don't worry, nothing will leave these four walls."

Subbu glances around to check if there are any cameras or other risky stuff, and when he is convinced it is safe to discuss, he explains our problem. "Doctor, we have a patient who will come to you with small injury or bruise. We need you to ask him a few questions about any recent accidents or injuries, check where they are, and write a regular prescription. The thing is, one of my boys will be acting as a mole and will be here to watch the entire scene. Can you do that?"

Subbu is direct and to the point. I think he knows this guy is surely going to help us. Subbu told me about his plan over the phone, and I was worried about the injury part because if our involvement somehow comes out in the open, we will be in big trouble. But he insisted that this is our best option, and the injury will be very small, with no long-term effects.

"Oh. That's easy. I thought you wanted more sinister stuff."

Oh. My. God. The kind of people in this world.

"No. That's about it."

"So, when do you want this to happen?"

"Today, in the evening."

"That's workable. And within my timings."

"I will send over my boy, who will coordinate with you."

"Sure."

"And your compensation?"

"I will discuss that over phone. I am sure big cheese Mr. Mehta will be thankful for my help."

He couldn't be more correct. Right now, big cheese Mr. Mehta wouldn't mind a big dent to his wallet.

With that, we part ways because Subbu needs to make

arrangements for the evening adventure. We decide to meet up late in the evening.

✦ ✦ ✦

The rest of the morning and all noon, I read about criminal cases where circumstantial evidence formed the basis of the verdict. Sanjay's guy, Sekhar, is efficient, with a good memory, and is able to help me research quickly. But the more I study, the more I realize that it's difficult to tilt the odds in our favour in the absence of direct evidence. Where there is no direct evidence, most often than not, the verdict had been challenged at a higher judiciary authority. Deep down, I have always known we run this risk but until we make some progress on this case, I cannot plan for my future defence.

Finally, late evening, Subbu calls. This time, he sounds very positive and excited over the phone, or maybe it's just me being hopeful. He comes trotting into my office with a pen drive and a bunch of papers.

As he enters, I look up at him and ask, "Where is your guy?"

"Hello to you too. He is not needed. I have got better stuff for you."

"Let's get started. I can't wait to know the outcome of your little adventure."

Subbu takes a seat and connects the pen drive to the laptop and an audio file begins to play. It's a conversation between Dr. Puri and another man, who I know is Jishnu.

"Hang on there. Let me take a look at your foot."

"Aahhhh."

The audio pauses for a few minutes.

"It appears to be a deep cut, but not to worry. Nothing a stitch or two won't fix. Just give me five minutes."

There is a noise of paper and tape and plastic, and Jishnu is wincing intermittently. After about fifteen minutes, I think the procedure is done, because Dr. Puri says, "There. It looks all right now. So, tell me, did you get a tetanus shot recently?"

"Yes. About four to five weeks ago."

"Oh. Generally, or did you get injured?"

"Hmm … a small injury in my calf. It's fully healed now."

"All right. Can I take a look at it?"

"Sure."

There is another pause, and then Dr. Puri speaks. "How did you get hurt? It looks like a metal cut."

"Yeah. Was a metal cut. A sharp corner grazed my leg when I was climbing down a metal staircase."

"Got it. Well, it's healed up well now. No need for another tetanus. But I will prescribe some iron supplements, a painkiller, and a short course of antibiotics. That should take care of everything."

"Okay. Thank you, Doctor."

The audio stops, and I release the long breath that I didn't realize I was holding. I keep staring at the screen in front of me, until Subbu shakes me from my reverie. "One more thing to make sure this is the right guy. The other guy, Laksh? It's not him. He has a strong alibi. Apparently, he had escorted his drunk friend out of the club when it was being evacuated and dropped him in his car. He drove the car to their house, put him to sleep there, and then slept there himself."

So, it's definitely Jishnu. But what's the motive?

"What about the eatery Vishal mentioned? Any information from there?"

"My boys are on the job. They are at that place right now. Since you mentioned Thursday evening, I thought someone who would normally be on that shift could help."

"Subbu, this is good. But every crime has a motive. Unless we find out what that is, our arguments will not hold water in the court. We need that."

"I will have something for you by tomorrow morning."

⁂

I head home for the night. This case is getting interesting by the day, and we are coming closer to the goal, but time is running out as well. Tara has requested for the hearing to be scheduled on Tuesday next week. She could wind up her work at Varanasi faster than we had estimated. I don't think Kishore Mehta can do anything this time. I still have my father to bank on as a last resort, but I know the risks involved with that.

And then there is the media. Two days ago, Nitya's mother had been hospitalized due to depression-induced weakness, and the Nari Shakti group berated the Indian legal system for delaying justice for an innocent victim. In a way, I am thankful for the fast progression of this case. I like this judge, who is reasonable and balanced. If pressure from the media mounts, there is a risk that the judge may be changed, and then all bets are off. I am hoping that doesn't happen.

This case is like playing Jenga. The tower is built on so many accurately placed blocks and is so fragile that the slightest imprecise movement could bring the entire structure tumbling down and cost us the game. Too many factors are playing a role in my success or failure here, and I am really worried about how they are piling up. One wrong move, even a small fallacious whisper, could cost Vishal his life.

CHAPTER 24

Ajay

The next day morning, I am eagerly waiting at Subbu's office to meet with his boys on their discovery about the happenings at the eatery. I reach earlier than the agreed time but fortunately, I have Subbu to keep me company. He tells me a little about how he got into this profession. After years of working with the CBI, he realized he had a penchant for crime investigation, but just like any other career, the climb to the top is brimmed with politics and games. Subbu got tired of playing and chose to start his own agency where he could be his own boss. He employs a group of street-smart but not academically proficient guys to do his site work and has a solid clientele.

I tell him about my experience with cybercrimes in Singapore and my work with Lawson Partners and how I came to be here. He is surprised that I am not a full-fledged criminal lawyer, and I am surprised that he hasn't researched *that* about me. Our conversation is interrupted when another one of Subbu's boys joins us with feedback from the eatery.

"Sir, I watched over the eatery from 5 p.m. to 10 p.m. yesterday. Thought speaking directly to the owner is risky so went after the waiters instead. There is one waiter, Gullu, who was willing to share some details, albeit for some payment. I agreed and he met me after his shift got over in the night.

"So, Jishnu and the girl were visitors at the eatery on Thursdays, when there is a 50 percent discount on the burgers. It's been their tradition for a long time. It's always Jishnu who pays for the meal. They grab their food and walk along the beach and sit near the rocks while chatting and eating their food. Gullu says they were good friends and were always at ease with each other. But this tradition stopped about six months ago and the two of them stopped going there. I asked him if there was any reason, maybe an altercation between the two.

"Gullu says the boy and the girl got into a fight with each other about six months ago. He doesn't know what they fought about, because he was not close enough to hear them completely, but he went out to check what was happening when he heard some loud noises coming from that direction. Apparently, the two of them got into a fight, and it appears that Jishnu tried to get physically intimate with her, maybe kiss her or something, and she slapped him and berated him for such debauched behaviour. Gullu is not very sure of the details, but it was clear that Jishnu tried something and the girl became furious at that."

"Is he willing to testify?" Subbu asks.

"Yes."

"It won't be enough."

Subbu turns to me, "Ajay, we have everything here. If this guy testifies, we can establish a motive as well."

This is what has been bothering me for days now. Whatever we have discovered can be easily challenged in the court.

"What we have is a set of unconnected events or information pockets that seemingly make a proof. Each one can be individually challenged and struck down. The judge may consider giving us more time to develop this further. But that's about it. We cannot be sure. I don't think this will even suffice to issue an arrest warrant against that guy. And if he is out loose, then he will tamper or seek refuge with one of these social groups who, in turn, will, accuse us of framing an innocent man."

"Then we have reached a dead end. Because there are no places to dig."

"Except there is."

"What is it?"

"I have an idea. But it may appear preposterous."

"I am listening."

"We need to get him to confess. Not by threatening. Not under duress. It must be suo-motto. Given freely. Because nothing, no damn force on this earth can challenge that. That's the ultimate proof."

Subbu stares at for a few moments and then asks. "Do you think we could stage a confrontation between Vishal and Jishnu that provokes Jishnu enough so that he spills the beans?"

I think about it for a while and then another idea strikes me. "No. I don't trust Vishal. He may lose his shit and strangle that guy the moment he sees him. I have another idea, but we need an ally."

Subbu considers me for a few seconds. The cogs are spinning in his head, and I think he knows what's on my mind. "The girl's brother."

"Yes."

"Do you know the risk involved? What if he turns against us?"

"He won't if we plan this carefully."

"Someone needs to speak to him. And I think it should be you."

"The moment he sees me, he will run in the other direction."

"No. There is something about you that makes people trust you and rely on you. You have a certain aura that makes so you damn convincing."

I laugh. "Thanks for the compliment."

"It was not intended to be one."

"Okay then. Thanks for rooting for me, even if I am the sacrificial lamb here. But anyway, I am up for it. What do we do next?"

Subbu gives me a confident smile, and I know we are going to make this happen.

✢ ✢ ✢

I am standing in the parking lot of Hydra Plastics Company waiting for my guest. It's about 7 p.m., and Subbu told me this is when he usually leaves work. I am a little nervous about this rendezvous, because I have never accosted anyone in my entire life.

The area is buzzing with employees pulling their vehicles out from parking slots or speaking to their loved ones about their day. I notice a familiar figure coming out of the lane lobby and walking towards the parking lot. I am wearing spectacles and a baseball cap to keep myself a little less conspicuous. There is a minute possibility that this adventure will lead to a physical attack by the man out there, for which I am fully prepared. I may be lean, but I am quite strong, thanks to my regular fitness regime. I can surely overpower the guy with a mean punch.

Niraj walks towards his bike parked near a tree and takes the keys out from his pocket. It's show time.

"Hello, Niraj."

He is startled at my voice. "What the hell are you doing here?"

"This is a public place, and I am surely not a terrorist or a criminal. I am a nobody or somebody just like you."

"You better be a nobody, because I don't want to have anything to do with you."

"You will. After you listen to what I have to say."

"I don't want to breathe the same air as you people who are out to exonerate my sister's killer!"

"How ironic! It is you who breathes the same air as him. Or even sometimes shares a meal."

Subbu has made sure nobody interrupts us during these precious few minutes by arranging dummy vehicles around us. I am thankful for his acumen and foresight because this conversation is going to turn even more bitter now.

"We can't talk about it here. But let me tell you, you are after the wrong guy. It's not Vishal. Your sister's killer is your friend Jishnu. But whether you believe me or not, please don't act or reveal anything about our little meeting to anyone because that will ruin any chances of justice your sister ever had."

I take his hand that's resting on the bike seat and slip my card into turn, and leave it.

⁘ ⁘ ⁘

I go home that night with a heavy head. It's not a new occurrence these days, since all I am able to think about is the case. The only source of happiness is my family. I need a distraction so badly that I am unwilling to be by myself even a for a short time. Thankfully, Tavi is home whenever I am back from work and the kids are spending more time with my parents. My kids call up their grandmother to check the day's menu and alter their place of dinner suitably.

But today, all of us are home. We ordered some takeout because my kids wanted to try out the new Mexican place that opened across the street. The tacos and salsa look delicious, and I am hungry from all the brain churning. Arka starts a football match on the big screen in our drawing room.

It's a UCL match between Barcelona and Chelsea, and with no goals scored on either side. We are about fifteen minutes late to the match but fully committed to watching it till the end. As the match progresses, the excitement and adrenaline rush slowly pull me in, and the lingering anxiety about Niraj almost disappears. Both teams have scored two goals, and now it's the penalty shots. My son and I are Barcelona supporters, and my son is a big fan of Messi. A few months ago, we went to France to watch a match where Messi was playing. One of the sponsors was my client who had accompanied us to the match, and we were given an opportunity to shake hands with the players. Arka was so ecstatic after shaking Messi's hands that he dreamily held his hands all night with adoration. The next morning, he told me that was the best gift I had ever given him, even better than the AI-enabled car racing set that I had bought for his fourth birthday. I felt ten-feet tall and frigging proud of myself that I could make it happen.

So now we are into the fourth penalty shot. Barcelona has an extra goal over Chelsea, and this one will mean a win for them. Every ounce of my attention is on the screen as Messi takes his position to hit the ball. Kepa, the opponent goalkeeper, has his eyes glued on Messi's foot and the ball. Messi takes a few steps back, angles his knee and at the last second, slightly tilts his foot to jettison the ball right into the top corner of the post, as Kepa pummels to his side expecting the ball to hit the side of the post instead.

What a fantastic and exquisitely executed deception!

Arka jumps on the couch in excitement and yells in victory. Later that night, as I am deep in contemplation, I realize what is happening with Vishal and us is pretty similar. This race is so close, and we are just a step away from winning. We all have our eyes on the target. But Niraj could change everything in a blink and throw our target forever away from us. He could inform the authorities or confide in Jishnu, or worse, go to the media. And then, it's all gone.

I cannot share the details of the case with Tavi owing to attorney-client confidentiality, but I broadly tell her about my predicament. She tells me about her recent experience with a patient here in India.

This patient had come to her for treatment of recurring pulmonary disorders and severe cough. As is the protocol she had always followed in Singapore, she looked over the medical history and figured out that the patient may be allergic to a certain hypertension medication he had been using. Obviously, it is the right thing to advise the patient to change the medication. But it is not as easy as it sounds. The medication had been prescribed by the head of the department in the hospital. There was a risk that this could be seen as rebellious behaviour. But my wife still did it, because she agrees with me that peace of mind and integrity are more valuable than career. She was fully prepared for a reprimanding action, but fortunately, her superior was an understanding guy who acknowledged the lapse in his prescription and immediately changed the medication.

A great man once said, 'If you want the right things to happen to you, you must always do the right thing.' I have done the right thing, and I am hoping the right thing will happen now.

CHAPTER 25

Ajay

The next day morning, I am getting ready for work when my phone buzzes. Since yesterday, any sound or activity on the phone has pushed my anxiety in anticipation that it could be Niraj. But unfortunately, again, it's Sanjay. He wants to know if our witness list is ready so he can submit it into court, as is required by the law. Actually, we are running quite a bit late, and it's not just a formality. But Sanjay says the court may consider if the judge allows it. I tell him that we may have to wait.

A few minutes later, my phone buzzes. I look at the clock—it must be my secretary. But when I pick up the phone, it's an unknown number. I immediately answer the call.

It's Niraj. He whispers a hesitant hello and I greet him back.

"Can we meet in about an hour?"

"Yes, sure. I will text you my office address. I will be waiting for you."

"Okay. See you then."

"See you soon. And Niraj, thank you for taking this leap of faith.

You are doing the right thing."

⋄⋄⋄ ⋄⋄⋄ ⋄⋄⋄

When I arrive at the office, my secretary takes me to the meeting room and tells me my guest is already there. He is earlier than the scheduled time. As I approach the meeting room, I see him through the glass walls. I think he has taken the day off today because he is in a casual t-shirt. He looks nervous and worried and is fidgeting. A wave of sympathy washes over me. This man has lost his sister and has now learnt that the person he considers his family could be her murderer. I cannot fathom anything happening to my family even in the wildest of my dreams, and I can only imagine Niraj's insurmountable grief.

When I open the door, he gets up and shakes hands with me.

"Can I offer you something to drink? "

"No. Thank you."

Subbu joins us right then and takes the chair next to me. But I stand up and walk over and take a seat closer to Niraj. Because I want him to know we are on the same side, and he is not alone in this.

"I have never handled a criminal case before. This is my first one. This is my first case in this country. I took this up because my family owes Kishore Mehta and because he trusts me."

Niraj is surprised at my admission of inexperience but doesn't stop me. I tell him this because I want him to know I am at a disadvantage too. I am making myself vulnerable to him so that he can trust me.

"I have been on the wrong path with this case for quite some time. I tried my best to prove Vishal's innocence. I would have continued on that path if not for Vishal. He came to me one night and told me that if the truth is not out, he would rather spend his life in prison as penance for not protecting the girl he loves and not giving her the justice she so deserves."

Again, Niraj blinks in disbelief but doesn't stop me.

"And that is when I knew he cares. That is when I knew I was wrong. And since then, a new journey began for all of us to find out the truth. Because if it's not Vishal, then who is it?"

Niraj shuts his eyes tightly and takes a deep breath, as if to ward off the all-consuming agony at the mention of his sister's death.

I continue after a pause. "That night, someone knocked on the door, and your sister opened it. The man pushed her back and stabbed her with the scissors. He locked Vishal in the bathroom till he arranged things and unlocked it when done. He hid behind the sofa and slipped into the bathroom when Vishal opened the door and came out. He finally escaped from the bathroom door. As they say, every crime leaves behind a clue. In this case, the man suffered an injury to his leg while rushing down the metal staircase installed on the outside wall. Subbu has investigated the evidence. and we found out it's Jishnu. We believe he loved your sister and wanted retribution when his affections were not returned. Your sister and Jishnu used to eat dinner at a food joint near the beach. The waiter there saw them arguing over something."

At this, Subbu plays a tape with the recorded conversation between Gullu and one of his boys. When the audio stops, Niraj slouches his shoulders and puts his head in his hands, and I can see his torso shaking. He is sobbing. But neither Subbu nor I make an attempt to comfort him. We just wait for him to compose himself and speak to us. After a while, he looks up. "I believe you. It is Jishnu."

Those are the most comforting words I have heard in the course of this case.

"When you accosted me that evening, my first thought was to grab the opportunity and avenge my sister. But then something about what you said struck me. You were so upfront and so specific about Jishnu. It didn't appear as if you were lying or trying to push for a settlement. So I went home and thought about it over and over again. That's when I recalled an incident. When I told Jishnu that Vishal and my sister had finally ended their relationship, he was unusually ecstatic. And now, he did not even attend my sister's last rites. We thought that was just his way of dealing with the situation. My mother has also complained that Jishnu has been furious with Nitya, saying all sorts of insensible things about her. Again, I assumed it was just some sort of depression. Jishnu had an abusive father and a miserable childhood. So his behaviour is sometimes different and ... violent.

It was, in fact, Jishnu who told me that my sister was having an affair. I cut short my trip, went to the college, and discovered them. He told me he had been following her and that's how he knew they were going to be there. I never suspected anything at that time. I always thought he was watching out for her safety and happiness. Now, when I piece things together, I realize how wrong I had been. I misread all those signals. I misjudged him completely."

"Its not your fault. Now that we know he's the culprit, we can finally seek justice for your sister."

"Can we prosecute him with this evidence? He has violent tendencies and is dangerous to society."

"I am afraid we cannot. There is a risk that it may be struck down as inadequate circumstantial evidence."

"Then what do you want to do?"

"Not us. It's you. Only you can take this to its right end. You have to help us, Niraj. More importantly, you have to help your sister."

"Anything to put that bastard behind bars. What can I do?" Niraj grits his teeth in barely contained fury.

"You need to make him confess."

Niraj doesn't respond. For the first time since we all assembled here, Subbu speaks up. "We have a plan. We need you on board with it. We need you to enact it."

"What kind of plan?"

"Niraj, Jishnu is psychologically affected by the abuse he suffered in his childhood. He is unstable. Such people are vulnerable and not equipped to handle provocative triggers. In fact, the murder he committed was not planned or premeditated. It was impulsive and an outcome of uncontrollable rage. He managed to be quick on his feet to figure out an escape and had an inordinate amount of luck on his side. I think he never expected your sister and Vishal to patch things up. And when they did, his frustration and fury spiralled out of control. That is exactly why he has no remorse for what he has done. He believes your sister was in the wrong and deserved to die. I am sorry to be so direct, but that's the cold truth."

"My sister was the daughter his mother never had! She cared about him so much. How could he be so heartless? How could he even think of such a gruesome act?"

I gently put my hand on his shoulders. Whatever has happened is indescribably cruel and unfortunate, and there is really nothing in this world that can measure up to the correct retribution. "I am truly sorry, Niraj. I am only hoping her soul will rest in peace once this guy is punished for his sins."

He takes a deep breath, shakes his head and says, "You mentioned a plan. What is it?"

"We believe he will confess to the murder if you provoke him. We need to stage it carefully. We are at an advantage, because he doesn't know that we have discovered his crime."

"But what if he doesn't? What if he denies any involvement?"

"He will at least give us clues, and we will need to think of something else then. But that's for later. For now, we have to plan this out. Are you okay to do it? There is a risk that he may try to harm you. We will make arrangements to curtail him. The police will have to be involved. I will speak to the DCP to arrange everything."

"I am not worried about my safety. I will risk my life. But I hope this plan works."

"It will. Because truth alone triumphs."

"When do you want to do this?"

"Before the next hearing the day after tomorrow. I think it should be tomorrow night. That way, we will be able to keep the media at bay for some time. If the arrest becomes public, it may again cause protests and delays. Let's meet in the evening to discuss the details."

The three of us part ways for the day, and Subbu promises to update me in the evening. I trust Subbu to deal with this properly. He is smart and shrewd and has an amazing acumen when it comes to criminal psychology.

Later that noon, I meet my father to give him a brief update on the case. He tells me he fully believes that Subbu can do the job, because he is like the Poirot of this city. He reminisces about how he met Subbu. Several years ago, my father was fighting for the junior Gupta brother who challenged the will of his father, which left the entire property to the older brother and not a single penny to the younger one. The junior Gupta believed that his father would never distribute the wealth unequally and would never treat him so unfairly. My father suspected foul play and suggested they hire an investigation agency to find out any tampering of the will or verify if the will was executed under duress. Since the junior Gupta could not afford expensive private detectives, they looked for someone smaller but talented. That's when the CBI passed on Subbu's contact to my father. Subbu had just started his business, and this client would be a big break for him in terms of reputation.

Subbu quickly got to the bottom of the situation and figured out that the father could potentially have been murdered. He arranged for the police to interrogate the older Gupta and as per Subbu's idea, the police threatened they knew about the contamination in the food based on the blood samples that had revealed traces of cyanide. That is when the culprit blurted out that there was no way that blood samples would reveal anything, because he used arsenic for poisoning, which is practically untraceable.

The team won the case and thus began my father's friendship and association with Subbu. My father used the latter's services on many occasions until he slowly diversified into new-age crime and corporate law. My father tells me that he started branching out into cybercrime and expanded the business in that direction because that was my forte, and he always hoped that I would come back to carry on his legacy.

Now I understand his actions of love, and I feel thankful and happy that he thought about me and my career—that he did, after all, care about me.

We also discuss his relationship with Kishore. He reminisces about his college days and how he bonded with Kishore during the summer break. He tells me that he would have slogged the summer making money if not for his foster-mother who insisted that he return home for a few days to spend time with the family. He is wistful and regretful as he talks about them and expresses his small satisfaction that, finally, he is able to do something for his brother.

CHAPTER 26

Ajay

I call up Subbu later in the evening, and he tells me that he has been in touch with Niraj to learn a bit more about Jishnu. Apparently, Niraj is aware of Jishnu's altercation with his mother's supervisor years ago.

Subbu tells me that Niraj is inviting Jishnu to the beach for a casual meeting, and they decide to execute the plan at that time and location. Subbu had also replayed the entire CCTV footage, this time focusing on Jishnu and his movements. The footage shows, he tells me, Jishnu watching someone on the dance floor very closely, and in hindsight, it must be the couple. He gets up a few times to refill his drinks. Subbu has surmised that Jishnu had something strong and was under the influence of alcohol that day. Also, while the footage clearly shows Jishnu getting up from his seat and walking to the opposite wall after the couple goes upstairs, that side of the club is a blind spot, so there are no feeds after that.

Subbu has unearthed some interesting information about Jishnu. He always suspected that the murderer had to be well acquainted with the club to move around and commit the murder so smoothly. And indeed, Jishnu knows the dance club very well. In fact, he was helping the club owner Toby on bookkeeping and other petty admin work a few weeks before the murder happened. He would go to the club twice or thrice in the evening for a couple of hours, do the job and get paid on a daily basis. Toby told Subbu that Jishnu was a super-smart chap.

And there is more—there are a few other people Subbu reached out to, who agreed that Jishnu had always followed Nitya. But they never suspected anything because they all thought he was watching out for her. But now it's clear that he was obsessed with the girl and whatever happened is the result of that obsession.

The entire next morning is spent preparing for the big evening. Subbu and his boys have planned everything to the last detail, including the location and the logistics. Sanjay is back in town and has managed to pull a few strings with the police to ensure they are undercover and hidden in strategic spots so that the entire scene can be viewed in person. Our guys have also arranged high-definition video cameras to record the entire conversation. A hidden microphone and a high-precision voice recorder are planted on Niraj's clothes. I have been advised to watch this from afar, on my laptop, where the whole sequence is being streamed real time. I am impressed with the arrangements and prudent use of technology, and I am hopeful that we are successful.

We assemble at our respective locations. I watch the entire sequence from the comfort of a small cabin some distance away from the main site. Niraj is already at the location and is waiting for Jishnu to join. He is carrying two cans of beer, and I am sure the one meant for Jishnu is spiked with something stronger. A few minutes later, Jishnu enters and both friends greet each other and sit down on the rocks. I observe Jishnu closely. He appears like any other guy. Not too tall but very lithe in stature. He has a dark-wheat complexion and a thick scruff covering his entire jaw. His hair is too long, and overall, his appearance is shabby and unrefined. He grabs the beer can that Niraj offers him and takes a big swig.

"Thanks for the beer, man. It's been a while since I had any alcohol. This feels so good."

"I know. Figured you may not have had time what with juggling so many jobs. How is your mother?"

"Like a mother hen! How is your mother?"

"Devastated. I don't think she will ever recover from the grief she is carrying."

"Don't worry. It will all be over tomorrow. That bastard is going to jail, and we will all be free from this fiasco."

"I hope so. But you know, they are big people. I am worried they may delay the case further."

"Not going to happen. The Nari Shakti group will move heaven and earth to ensure that the verdict is delivered tomorrow. Besides, I heard the public prosecutor is one hell of a woman and no match for the douchebag of a lawyer they hired."

"Yeah. That she is."

"That bastard Vishal will rot in hell. If it were up to me, I would ensure a terribly painful slow death for him."

Jishnu practically grits his teeth and his uncontained fury is clearly visible in his expressions. He looks dangerous. That sneering laugh, the disdain in his tone, those eerie eyes. The tell-tale signs are all there. I wonder why Niraj couldn't see it earlier.

"Vishal getting arrested is justice for my sister, but I know it is not enough. Because she did not deserve this in the first place. She was so pure, so innocent, always putting others first, always thinking about others."

"Well, she was not as innocent as you think. You remember how they used to spend hours together all those months ago. I told her many times not to get too close to that guy. But she never listened. Stupid, stupid girl!"

"Don't say that! She made a promise to me that she would never see him again. I know her, Jishnu. She would never break a promise she made to me."

"Oh God! You are so naïve, just like her. Do you think it's easy to resist the charm of a wealthy, handsome bastard like Vishal? She might have promised you many things, but trust me, she never kept her promise. Once the guy came back running to her, she went right back. That's why she happily danced with him that night and followed him to the room. Like a puppy after a bone."

I am sure Niraj is seething with rage at these outright insults thrown at his sister. How difficult it must be to control his anger! But he never loses control and plays along.

"Bullshit! You always say that about Nitya. But I know her. My sister is an angel. She would never do anything that would anger me. You just don't know anything, you idiot! You are always too deep in your books to even know what's going on around you."

"All you people think I am dumb about these things. You, my mother, even your sister. The truth is that you guys never knew my value. Your sister is no exception. She never realized how much I loved her. How much I cared for her. All she saw was that fucking flashy Vishal, with his expensive car and branded shades. She was a gold-digger, just like all the other girls!"

"What are you saying, Jishnu! Of course she loved you. She loved you like a brother. And look at you. Do you think you are easy to love? Nitya would never go after money. She genuinely believed Vishal was a nice guy."

Jishnu laughs at that hysterically. "Vishal is a nice guy? Really? Do you know how many times he had seduced her? How many times they were physically intimate? They would make out in secret places. In the college storeroom. In his car. In dark corners in our campus corridor. Oh God! My stomach would churn whenever I saw them together doing all those disgusting things. And you think they are both innocent little children."

"Those things happen in love, Jishnu. But Nitya would never go too far and cross the line. She was very socially conscious and responsible."

"You are so very wrong. Your sister bought a contraceptive pill in the afternoon before the party. Now, why would any girl buy that?"

"Just stop this nonsense, you moron. She bought migraine pills. Don't make things up! You are blowing it out of proportion and baselessly shaming my sister."

"I am not shaming her any more than she has shamed herself. Your sister is no angel. She is a whore, who jumped at the first opportunity to get into bed with that lecherous bastard. You should have seen them that night. They just could not control themselves. They were all over each other. My skin crawled and my insides churned at the sight of them together."

At this, Niraj's eyes go wide and he looks at him with shock and rage written all over his face. Jishnu realizes what he has blurted out and hastily gets up to leave. But Niraj grabs his collar in a tight grip. "How do you know all this? How the hell do you know she bought a contraceptive pill?"

"Nothing. I don't know anything."

"You vile, sick bastard! You were following her, weren't you? How else would you know these things? You turned out just like your father!

A vile monster who derives sadistic pleasure out of …"

Niraj is not able to finish that sentence, because Jishnu grabs his neck and starts to strangle him.

"Yes! I am like my father. Who else would I be? Your sister said the same thing to me when I proposed to her, you know? That bitch. She deserved to die! I was finally at peace when I twisted the scissors in her throat and watched the blood ooze from her neck. It was a sight to behold, seeing her writhe under my hands. She *deserved* to die! You all deserve to die."

From my laptop, I can see the situation worsening. I quickly close the machine and rush to the site. But DCP Raghuram has already reached the scene with another cop, and the two of them pull Jishnu away from his victim. He is cuffed and arrested and taken to the police jeep. He keeps screaming and yelling and kicking his legs, "Leave me, you idiots! Let me go!"

Subbu holds a nearly collapsing Niraj and calls for an ambulance. In a few minutes, paramedics arrive and escort him to the hospital. Subbu tells me he will be fine and ready to testify tomorrow. The police team collects samples of the evidence, the video feeds, takes photographs and leaves. Subbu and I are left alone at the beach.

We take a short walk, closer to the water and watch the waves at our feet. Subbu throws light on a couple of aspects of what happened. When he spoke to Niraj and enquired more about Jishnu's childhood and personality, he realized that his father had always been a difficult topic, and the mention of his father always triggered anger and agony in him. When Jishnu was a child, he was mocked by a classmate regarding his father and Jishnu, in a fit of rage, hit the boy with a duster multiple times. The teacher who withheld Jishnu complained to his mother about the incident. His mother was aware of Jishnu's weakness and always avoided the topic of his father, but never actually dealt with it by taking him to a psychiatrist. They never had the resources or the awareness to take any remedial action. The night of the murder, Jishnu dumped his blood-stained t-shirt somewhere and came home only in his vest. His mother had since been looking for the lost t-shirt.

We congratulate each other on the job well done and I request Subbu to come over to the court tomorrow to see in action the fructification of all his efforts. He agrees and leaves to catch some much-needed rest.

The sea is not too aggressive today. I have always felt at peace when I come here. My mother always told me, the sea, the moon, and the face of one's progeny always bring happiness to our hearts and push away our sorrows. I thought it was just a metaphor, until I actually experienced the first two when I was a child and the last when I became a father.

Today again, the sea brings a calm over me. So much could have gone wrong, and we took a huge risk with the whole plan, possibly endangering Niraj's life. But we succeeded in the end. My thoughts drift to my grandmother's painting in my room.

"Protect the truth and the truth will protect you."

CHAPTER 27

Ajay

I have never been too religious in my life. I do perform the rituals—my mother and my wife request me to—but I am not overly involved in any of those. Most often than not, my mind is somewhere else, and I am only physically present.

My father always told me a man makes his own fate and no power in this universe can change that. But Tavi believes karma is a cycle that plays on a person's conscience, and Yoga helps a person have power on that conscience. My mother has blind faith in God and in higher purpose.

Over the years, I have become more tolerant of beliefs and practices concerning providence and a higher force, and more empathetic to traditions and religion. I listen to other spiritual theories only out of intellectual curiosity. That's about it.

But today, I feel different. I realize now that whatever has happened is not just because of me. It's because a set of people believed in the truth and believed in themselves to discover it, with an untainted and committed mind. And that happened because we had the right collective conscience and strength of character. All of us had to be in our right minds to have come to this stage. Subbu always told me this murder was an outcome of an impulse, and since there was no preparation and premeditation, it was near impossible to trace it. Which means that if Vishal had not confronted me the other day and if I had not introspected, we wouldn't have connected with Subbu or reached out to Niraj. All this would not have happened.

And that's why I beckon the power of truth again to help justice prevail and let us emerge victorious.

My father and my wife are waiting for me in the drawing room when I enter. They both look happy and proud. I am yet to bring it all together, but they don't seem to acknowledge that important detail. That's family. They are proud because they know I have done my best. The result doesn't matter.

We all drive to the court together, and my father and Tavi engage in a carefree conversation about schools in India. I feel happy seeing them talk like this, with no inhibitions or fear of judgement. They are not a successful lawyer and an ambitious doctor. They are neither father of the man and wife of the man. They are just two people in a family.

I look out the window and see the court building approaching. My father once told me that the court exemplifies the absolute power of truth and is thus invincible. And that's why it's built in such a way that it's very sight and presence must remind people of their smallness before such power. And it's true. As I look up at this temple of justice, I am humbled and left penitent.

On our way to the court, we spot Tara walking towards us. She and my father exchange respectful greetings with one another. Last night, Subbu briefed Kishore Mehta about what happened, and he was happy to know we had made such amazing progress. He immediately made arrangements to keep the media at bay and provided us with top security to ensure we are not bothered until the case is concluded. My father, on his part, used his influence to convince the judge to complete the hearing in one sitting.

So now, all of us are assembled here to fight the last step in achieving liberation. The judge enters the hall and after the protocol formalities, instructs us to commence our arguments. Tara goes first.

"Your Honour, the Honourable Court, during the last hearing, granted additional time for the respective parties to gather any additional evidence or take into account any new developments in respect of this case. I humbly submit that no new developments have taken place since then and no new evidence has been admitted. Taking into account the evidence verified and confirmed so far, I appeal to the Honourable Court to convict Mr. Vishal Mehta, the accused in this case, with charges of sexual abuse and murder, and sentence him under sections 35 and 36 of the Indian Sexual Abuse Act. That's all, your Honour."

"Mr. Bhargav, do you have anything to say?"

I stand up, walk towards the judge and address him. "Your Honour. I must first express my gratitude to the public prosecutor for opening my eyes. Because she had asked this very pertinent and paramount question, 'If not Vishal, who killed Nitya Harde?' If not for that, I would not be standing here today, presenting to you the truth.

"Your Honour, the human mind thrives on spontaneity and impetuosity, because that's the way it functions and conserves resources for more cardinal problems. We hope in haste and despair in haste. We believe in haste; we betray in haste. We grieve in haste and rejoice in haste. We attach motives in haste and provide excuses in haste. Let's say, we find that the milk pan we left on the table is now half empty. Our first suspect is the neighbour's cat but never our own folks.

"And that's exactly what has happened here. There was a crime, and there was a rich man. Our mind discredited all other possibilities and immediately attached a motive to that man and accused him of that crime. But today, I am here to rectify that, Your Honour. And to that end, I would like to present my first witness, Mr. Gullu Govind."

"Objection, Your Honour. Who is Mr. Gullu Govind, and how is he relevant to the case? Mr. Bhargav never shared any witnesses and new witnesses may not be admitted at this crucial juncture of the case."

"Your Honour. During the last hearing, Mrs. Rathod presented the testimony of a new witness, citing their importance to the case, and added that I would be given an opportunity to cross-examine later. I appeal to the Honourable Court to extend the same concession to me as well. And maybe the public prosecutor will not have any need for cross-examination after I present my evidence."

"Objection overruled. Please continue."

Gullu enters the court and looks clueless but excited. I think he will enjoy the attention and limelight he is going to be smothered with after this case is over. After he takes his oath, I ask him, "Mr. Govind, do you know Ms. Harde? And if so, how?"

"Sir, she used to come to our food joint with her friend Jishnu very often. I have known her for about two years now."

"Can you describe the nature of her relationship with Jishnu?"

"Objection, Your Honour. The defence here is trying to defame the girl!"

"Objection overruled. Please continue."

"They were good friends. But I think Jishnu was in love with her. One day, I saw them fighting about something. I was watching them from afar, but it was clear that Jishnu tried to get physically close to her and she refused. He got a bit assertive, and she slapped him."

"Thank you. Your Honour, now I would like to call Mr. Niraj Harde to the witness box."

"Objection, Your Honour. Mr. Bhargav is steering the case in an altogether new and irrelevant direction. Who is Jishnu? And Mr. Niraj was already thoroughly cross-examined."

"Your Honour. It is indeed a new direction, but it is the right direction. And I am not going to cross-examine Mr. Harde. He is here for a new testimony as you will now see."

Niraj approaches the witness box. He looks tired and defeated and has a bruise around his throat. Subbu assured me that he insisted on testifying, although he suffered some damage to his vocal cords. He swears on the book and smiles at me.

"Mr. Harde, I am sorry for your injury. Can you tell us how it came to be?"

"I was attacked by Jishnu last night."

"Your Honour, can Mr. Bhargav enlighten us as to who Jishnu is?" Tara interjects

She is clearly impatient and seething with restlessness, so I put her out of her misery. "Your Honour. As you will see in some time, Jishnu Savarkar is Ms. Harde's killer."

At my announcement, there is pin-drop silence in the court, followed by hushed whispers. Tara is shell-shocked, and I continue with full confidence.

"So, Mr. Harde, why did Mr. Savarkar attack you?"

"I met Mr. Savarkar at the beach yesterday. We discussed what's happening in our lives right now, and I expressed my despair over what happened to my sister, who was innocent. He disagreed with me and argued vehemently that my sister was a gold-digger and was promiscuous, and that she was having an affair with Vishal. The argument spiralled out of control and Jishnu admitted to following my sister and knowing her whereabouts on the night she died. I was furious at his vile behaviour and confronted him. He could not control his rage. He tried to choke me and admitted that he murdered my sister!"

This time, there are loud whispers in the courts until the judge orders silence.

"Thank you, Mr. Harde. You may go now."

"Your Honour. Now, I would like to present a video recording of what happened yesterday between Mr. Harde and Mr. Savarkar."

The judge gives approval, and the video starts to play. Tara has her hand over her head in regret over whatever has happened. I see Vishal sitting right behind. He is watching the entire scene intently as tears gather at the corners of his eyes. Kishore Mehta is shaking his head at the monstrosity of the crime. My father and Tavi are looking at me to gauge my emotions. Subbu is intently viewing the fruit of his work, with a look of confidence and resignation on his face.

CHAPTER 28

Ajay

"Your Honour. Now I would like to call Mrs. Savarkar, Jishnu's mother, to the witness box."

This is Subbu's last-minute addition to the case. Last night, when the DCP informed Jishnu's mother about the arrest, the lady broke down and cursed her son and his stupid reckless mind that could connive and commit such a heinous crime. Subbu expected the lady to fight back, but she dejectedly admitted that her son had distorted tendencies, and she was truly sorry that she could not save Nitya from such a horrendous fate. She was more than willing to testify against her son.

So now she is here - frail and lost and tormented as she approaches the witness box. She folds her hands in contrition and remorse.

"Mrs. Savarkar. Do you believe that your son killed Ms. Harde?"

She sobs uncontrollably for a few minutes and finally speaks up. "Yes. Whatever Niraj says may be true. My son had a horrible childhood, sir. He was brutally beaten and humiliated by his own father. That left him disturbed and scarred. Even today, when someone mentions his father, he becomes wildly angry and violent. The two of us were barely surviving until we met the Harde family. Nitya's mother, Radha, is a goddess of a woman. She took us in, found a job for me and encouraged Jishnu to go to school. Niraj and Nitya were always kind to my son, and they were the only friends he ever had. They never treated him differently and always had his back. My son had always been possessive about Nitya, always worried whenever she talked to other boys. I knew he cared for the girl but told him to not have any hopes of romance with her, because she clearly treated him as her brother. But he never heeded my advice. That idiot. And now look what he has done. I lost my daughter because of my son. It's all my fault. I should have raised him better!"

The lady is weeping and inconsolable, and finally, she is taken away by the attenders.

"Your Honour. I request the permission of the court to present DCP Raghuram Dhawan, the officer on duty for this case."

"Permission granted. Please proceed."

"Thank you, Your Honour."

DCP Raghu enters the witness box and takes the oath.

"DCP Dhawan, please tell us about what happened after yesterday."

"After we watched Jishnu Savarkar choking Mr. Niraj Harde, we arrested him immediately, took him into our custody and interrogated him at the police station."

"What did Mr. Savarkar tell you?"

"Mr. Savarkar was in shock and denial initially, but eventually confessed to committing the murder, after we replayed the video of his confrontation with his friend. Jishnu had always been in love with Ms. Nitya Harde and had made a habit of following her every move. We found a picture of Ms. Harde in his wallet. He apparently stole and kept her cosmetics in his room.

"He was furious that she was having an affair with Vishal and separated the couple by informing her brother about their clandestine affair. He was ecstatic when the couple split up and expressed his feelings to Nitya. When she rebuffed his advances, he could not deal with the rejection and tried to force himself on her. He even admitted to following her and informing her brother. Nitya was disgusted with his actions and warned him to stay out of her life. He let it go temporarily but decided to pursue it again after a while.

"He kept following her around and figured out that the couple had rekindled their romance. He was furious that Nitya was back with Vishal. Their physical intimacy, which he watched without being noticed, only fuelled his rage. When he saw Nitya buying the contraceptive pill, he realized that the couple were up to something that night. His original plan was to catch the couple red-handed and beat up Vishal. He was keeping a close eye on the couple and tiptoed to the stairwell and crawled up the stairs.

He watched the couple from the glass panel, and when Vishal went to the bathroom, he knocked on the door. When Nitya opened, he was overcome with fury at the sight of her, and in a fit of rage, he kicked the door close with his foot, pushed her against the desk and stabbed her. Soon enough he realized what he had done and figured out he needed to escape. That's when his mind hatched a plan. He partially locked Vishal's bathroom door, pushed Nitya to the couch, wiped off the scissors with his handkerchief to destroy his fingerprints, opened the top button on her jeans and slipped them down her hips to make it look like a rape case. He then hid behind the sofa. Once Vishal came out, his first instinct was to save the girl, and he didn't notice anything that was happening around him. That served to Jishnu's advantage, and he could easily slip into the bathroom. Once inside, he looked around and saw the openable vent with the handle and realized he could get out. Again, the metal scaffold came to his rescue, and he got out and jumped a few feet to grab the railing and fled home. He dumped the t-shirt somewhere and told his mother that the t-shirt had been missing for days. We have his entire confession recorded for the court's record and consideration."

"Thank you, DCP Raghu. Your Honour, I request your permission to summon Jishnu Savarkar to the witness box."

"Permission granted."

Jishnu approaches the witness box. His hands are cuffed, and he looks solemn as he enters the box. I don't think there is a trace of remorse on his face or even a trace of fear or grief about the gravity of his situation. It is as if he has resigned to his fate. He refuses to take an oath on any book and swears to speak the truth. This time the judge addresses him.

"Mr. Savarkar. The evidence and your confession clearly speak for the crime you have committed. Do you have anything to say in your defence?"

"No."

"Do you admit to murdering Ms. Nitya Harde?"

"Yes."

"Mrs. Rathod, do you have any objections?"

"No, Your Honour," Tara sighs and responds in resignation.

The judge writes down something and finally pronounces the judgement. "After taking into account the evidence presented, examined and analysed so far and taking into account the statement of DCP Raghuram Dhawan, the court hereby pronounces Mr. Jishnu Savarkar guilty as charged with the murder of Ms. Nitya Harde. Under sections 35 and 36 of the Indian Penal Code and Section Offences

Act, 2003, the court awards life sentence to Mr. Jishnu Savarkar. He may be taken into police custody immediately. The Honourable Court also acquits the previously accused Mr. Vishal Mehta, and all charges against him stand nullified with immediate effect. The case is hereby closed, and the court is adjourned."

Once the judge leaves, there is loud applause and happy clapping in the room. I look around to see Vishal sink to his seat as the Mehta couple engulf him in a tight embrace. But I can see he is warring with his own emotions—not sure whether to be happy that he has been given another opportunity at life or to grieve the unfortunate and horrendous murder of his girlfriend. As I approach him, Mrs. Mehta looks up and takes my hand in both of hers in a gesture of deep gratitude, and Kishore Mehta clasps my arm in admiration and thankfulness. I then go to my family. Tavi gives me a quick hug, and Subbu comes near us and pats my back in a friendly, congratulatory gesture. Out of the corner of my eye, I can see Sanjay giving me a thumbs up.

I am happy with the reactions of people around me, but it is the unmistakable elation and pride on my father's face that profoundly moves me. He gives me a smile and nod and hesitantly opens his arms. I go to him freely and truly embrace him for the first time ever in my life. He whispers words of pride and happiness in my ears.

We turn to see Kishore Mehta approaching us. He takes my father's hands in gratitude. "You have raised one hell of a boy, Vikram. God bless him. And thank you for helping out this pitiful excuse of a brother that I am. I cannot express how much this means to me."

"You are welcome, Kishore. But don't be a stranger anymore. You are my brother, after all."

"I will never forget that again. Let me go talk to Niraj. We both need each other to heal."

I appreciate Kishore Mehta's gesture. He is right; all of them need to heal and move on.

For the first time since my coming to India, I let the ecstasy of this victory and an excitement about my future wash over me. I drown myself in these enervating emotions. They say that one's misfortune could be another's opportunity, and what has happened with me is something similar. This case made me forge valuable relationships with new people, gave me new friends and allies, brought me back to my country, and mended my relationship with my father. But most of all, it reminded me that truth is indeed absolute. My eye catches the text on the pamphlet Tavi is carrying in her hands:

Asatoma Satgamaya

Tamasoma Jyotirgamaya

Mrityorma Amirtangamaya

Om shanti shanti shanti.

(From untruth to truth

From darkness to light

From death to eternity

Let there be peace, peace, peace.)

EPILOGUE

Vishal

I sit on the edge of my seat, anxious and excited. All my attention is on the presenter on the stage in front of me. My film has been nominated for the Oscars, as India's nomination for the Best Film in the Foreign Language Category—the most prestigious recognition a film could ever get. It has done extremely well in India too, despite the absence of song and dance sequences and the heavy usage of the English language. I am the youngest film director in Bollywood and perhaps the youngest ever to be nominated for the award.

My film, *Fury of the Storm*, is about a divorced couple trapped in a storm and a rescue officer from the army who desperately tries to locate them. In this adversity, the couple rediscovers love and faith, and the army officer finally finds peace and closure. I spent a great deal of time with the army to study their rescue efforts, and this cinema is the essence of my learnings from that period.

❖ ❖ ❖

After the case was closed and the ordeal buried, everybody moved on with their lives. My father gained all the more reputation because he had a brave and righteous son. My mother was ecstatic and now more empathetic towards the less privileged. Ajay settled in India to crack some prestigious and challenging cases. Subbu quietly carried on with his work. My friends were back to their old lives, and I scraped through my college exams and ended up with mediocre grades.

But mentally, I could not move on. It was as if time stopped for me the night of Nitya's death. The grief and agony were so all-consuming that I became helpless, hopeless, and lifeless. Nothing caught my interest. Going to bed was a scary task because of the nightmares that would keep me awake and sweaty all night. I lost weight and became a shell of my former self. Music sometimes gave me solace, but whenever I heard a familiar tune, the sound of Nitya's beseeching voice would echo and dissipate around my entire being.

My worried parents finally took me to a shrink who prescribed sleep medication but wisely advised me that the pills were a solution, not a cure. The cure had to come from within me. I just needed to unearth it.

Our family became very close to the Bhargav's, and Ajay became a brotherly figure in my life. I spent a lot of time with his adorable kids and longed for a family like his. But deep down, I was not sure if I could ever love again, for the fear of loss had seeped into every corner of my being.

During one of our customary dinners, Tavishi suggested I meet Sadhguru to seek a solution. I had never been spiritual or religious in my life, but I was willing to try even the whackiest of ideas, so I agreed. Surprisingly, Sadhguru was very understanding of my pain and very convincing in his counsel. He suggested that to heal myself, I should heal others. Because our mind sometimes forgets a course of action and must be reminded. Tavishi told me that sometimes, infants can't sleep because they simply don't know that they must close their eyes. So, the mother often looks into their eyes and closes her own eyes to get them to sleep.

And that's how my journey and rebirth began. I enlisted myself as a volunteer in the rescue team for the ongoing floods in Kerala. The wrath of nature was so vast in comparison to the curse of my fate. I did everything, right from lifting people and feeding children to cleaning floors and building houses. The experience was riveting and humbling. When I came back home, I was determined to tell the world about my experiences and decided to make a film.

Today, when the presenter announces the winner, Mr. Vishal Mehta, my face splits into a huge grin. My parents lock me in a tight embrace and as I walk to the stage, Ajay pats my back in a gesture of pride and happiness. I accept the award and look at the audience, and I realize this is my first and biggest achievement. I feel blessed and fortunate that after all that I lost, fate did revive me and managed to give me the spirit and vigour to fight back and reclaim my life.

I am standing in front of the hibiscus tree on my college campus, now called the Souffle Adda by my juniors. I have been invited to play the guitar for the Twenty-Fifth College Day celebrations. This tree was planted by my bandmates as a homage to the spirit of my first love, Nitya. She always loved the hibiscus flowers—they are simple, with just five petals and a single lanky stalk, yet beautiful. I am listening to the song *Breaking Ties* by Oceanlab, which she was so fond of back then. The earphones belong to her; they are the only memory of hers that I have kept with me.

After the case was closed, Niraj and I developed a friendship of sorts, because we both shared the loss of the girl we loved. We would check on each other now and then and offered to help each other, however we could. My father offered to pay the family a hefty amount to take care of his mother's medical expenses, but he flatly refused, and I respected that about him.

He got married a couple of months ago but did not invite me. I knew why. But I still surprised him at the wedding. He was ecstatic that I had come over and profusely apologized, saying he was hesitant to call a celebrity for his wedding. I was happy he had done very well for himself. I did karaoke at the wedding and had a lot of fun. It was simple yet happy, and I always made it a point to be at happy places.

Now, I take the earphones into my hands, fond and wistful. These were actually my earphones, which I had given to Nitya many years ago. She always refused gifts from me so I couldn't buy her anything. One day, she grabbed my earphones to find out what I was listening to and was surprised at the quality of the sound. So, I asked her to keep it for a while.

Months after the case was closed, Niraj called me one day to tell me that he was distributing all of Nitya's items to an orphanage for children. I asked him if I could have something to keep as a memory. When I went to their home and looked around her room, my eyes landed on these earphones, and I immediately asked if I could take them with me. Niraj understandingly obliged. They have been with me since.

I get into my car and drive to the beach as I listen to *Feelings* by *Chainsmokers* playing softly on my music system. I park my car and walk towards the water when I spot a college kid happily singing aloud this same song.

I take that as a cosmic sign.

He is lost in his own world and looks blissful with his eyes closed and head bobbing from side to side. I tap his shoulder, and he jumps.

"Want these?"

He eyes the object in my hand. When he sees the brand, he takes them with a happy smile.

I walk away before he can even thank me. I have given away her earphones because it's time to let them go.

It's time to let her go.

I walk towards a shadow waiting for me. As if she can hear my footsteps in the sand, she turns around and wraps her arms around my waist.

"I love you."

I smile and place a soft kiss on her lips. "I love you too. So much."

Her eyes widen in surprise at my words because I have never said them before. I am finally able to say it.

Because it is the truth.